Cryptid Pursuits #1

Skunk Ape Kingdom

By Matt Betts

2023 Deathbot Books

Dedication

This is for all those writers that keep on encouraging me and laughing *with* me, rather than *at* me.

1

The window of a nearby patrol car shattered as special agent Eli Millet approached the scene. He ducked his head down lower and crouched to stop next to the only familiar face that caught his eye.

"Gino, this doesn't look like it's going well. What's the situation?"

State Trooper Gino Mathis grimaced before shaking Eli's hand. "Not a whole heap different than it was when we talked earlier. Ludlow Falls Bank and Trust. Robbery gone wrong. Four suspects inside, we're thinking three males and one female. All wearing masks. We have three customers, one bank guard and four employees stuck inside."

"Eight hostages?"

Gino nodded. "That's the long and the short of it."

It wasn't Eli's first bank robbery; he'd been with the FBI for far too long to have escaped that part of the job. He'd worked with Gino on a bank robbery before, but those were arrested without incident as they exited a bank up the road aways.

"Anyone injured?"

"Not sure. The clerk at the Dollar Bonanza across the street heard shots and called us."

Eli peered around the side of the police van and assessed the scene. The blinds were all drawn and closed, the doors were covered with a shade, so there was no real way to see in. The one exception being the lone pane of glass they'd punched out in order to shoot at the police or anyone else that got close. It was maybe three feet by three feet, and big enough for a skinny cop to climb through. The officer would have to be fairly thin and not wearing a lot of gear. The skinny part ruled out Millet and he knew it. He wasn't completely out of shape, but there was no way he was getting through the gap quickly.

A hole at the top of one of the windows caught his eye. "Is that a bullet hole up near the top of the glass there? Maybe they were shooting into the air?"

"Could be. Warning shots? Their effort to get their hostages to understand they were serious about what they were doing?"

It was Eli's assessment as well. It was a move criminals learned from television and the movies. *Everyone put your hands in the air, this is a robbery. Blam!* Of course, the announcement was usually followed by the declaration that if the people did as they're told, no one would get hurt. It was a confusing and misleading chain of sentences, to say the least.

It turned quiet after the volley greeting Eli's arrival. Maybe because there weren't any exposed targets for the suspects to shoot at, or maybe because they'd made their point about shooting at anything that moved.

"Sniper?"

Gino nodded and motioned to the hotel across the street. "Only one. And she's on the second floor over there. Set up on the restaurant patio. Scared the hell out of the tourists having brunch over there, but I think some kid asked for her autograph before they evacuated the place."

"The gunfire didn't already have them concerned?"

"I don't know. The omelets are pretty good over there. Maybe they were just savoring the taste."

It came back to Eli then how laid-back Gino had been the last time. He seemed almost too calm then, even as the situation reached the tense moments before those particular criminals gave up. Maybe it was something Eli hadn't figured out yet in the crazy world of law enforcement. Not that Eli was nervous or amped up at a crime scene, he wasn't comfortable being shot at.

Eli looked around at how light the sheriff's team was. There were two patrol cars from the city police stopping traffic a few blocks in any direction, a couple of sheriff's cars in front of the bank and the SUV they were currently using for a command post. Until more help arrived, they were going to be spread pretty thin.

"You have more people on the way?" Eli asked.

Gino nodded. "I have a call in to the Tallahassee SWAT, but they're still a ways out. Nasty accident out on the highway. Most of our people were working with the highway patrol on that when this went down."

"The bureau's tactical team is en route, but I'm guessing we have 45 minutes or so till they hit town. It seems like a busy day in Florida for law enforcement."

Gino's radio buzzed with sudden chatter. "Yeah?"

A voice on the other end came through clearly. "One of the male suspects has been lingering at the window an awful lot. I can get a clear shot."

"Okay, hold."

If they took the man in the window out, it would leave the other three to retaliate however they wanted. Killing hostages would be at the top of their list.

"Wait them out?"

"That's my plan. At least for the time being. Now, if any of them get better at aiming and start hitting people, things will have to change, of course," Gino said. "Of course, if these jackasses keep shooting up the town from inside, maybe they'll run out of ammunition and decide to give up."

"I would like that outcome, as well." Eli thought it was strange no one inside reached out with demands, or started negotiating a way out yet. Gino said earlier the cops had established a phone link to the inside, but nobody answered their calls. A dialogue with the suspects would go a long way to figuring out the general mood and mindset inside the building. Otherwise, it was just a bunch of cops staring at a building and guessing about things.

"Well." Eli pulled a package of gummy bears out of his jacket pocket and tore them open. "I suppose if we're waiting, I have time for breakfast?"

"I thought you were a health nut," Gino said.

Eli could feel his face redden. "I was… I AM… but my kids leave their snacks everywhere. Sometimes they make their way into my car, or jacket or whatever."

"Sure, they do." Gino sat on the bumper of the vehicle and sipped from a metal mug. "My damn kids keep leaving their coffee and bear claws laying around and I have no choice but to consume them."

There was never any doubt in Eli's mind Gino could actually live off of donuts and caffeine. The man was a walking action movie cliche–loose tie, balding, with a thick bushy mustache beneath his nose. When they'd previously crossed paths, Eli had recently begun a diet and exercise regimen to cut out the sugary foods and drinks. It was all he could do not to take the various pastries Gino continuously offered. In fact, he was pretty sure he gained five pounds through osmosis.

"And I wouldn't say, health NUT exactly. I'm an enthusiast of staying fit, I guess."

"Whatever." Gino already had another pastry in his hand, different from the one before. It was like he was a donut magician pulling rabbits out of a hat.

2

Inside the bank, Lana Dodd sat on the floor with her back against the teller's desk. "This is messed up. This isn't how it was supposed to go."

"No shit." Ricky G said. "We all figured it out already. What took you so long?"

In the corner by the manager's office, a pool of blood gathered under the bank guard's body. She'd tried to help him, but he'd been shot in the chest and there was nothing she could do. The other three didn't seem to give a damn. They were more concerned with how much money they could grab and then they worried about how they were going to escape. It was far too late to think about it once they'd filled the bags with cash.

They'd done this before. Twice in Louisiana and once in Mississippi. All of those previous heists had gone smoothly from start to finish, but that was before her uncle brought on Ricky G, the muscle. He was certainly not the brains of the operation, more of a shoot first and then shoot again type of addition to the crew.

A bead of sweat formed on Lana's temple and she reached up to wipe it away. She knew what they were doing was wrong. Each and every time she told herself it was the last time. They had enough money, and they only had so much luck to last them the rest of their lives. Eventually, they'd come across a guard who didn't lay down on the floor, or a customer carrying a concealed weapon or something equally as likely to get them caught or shot. And here was the day.

"Where is your damn brother?" Hank Marx asked.

"If he's smart, he's a hundred miles from here by now," Lana said. "Just because he's driving the getaway car, doesn't mean he's obligated to get caught with us." Her brother, Danny, was one big reason she was still doing the stupid jobs. He would do whatever Hank said, because he was family. And Hank wasn't exactly one to reciprocate. He was in it for himself, without much care for anyone else. Never in a million years would Lana have guessed she'd be robbing banks with her uncle, two ex-cons and her brother if you'd asked her in high school. She was on her way to an art school in Washington, at least that's where she'd applied. Even got accepted, but when it came time to pay tuition, the money just wasn't there. No matter how many extra shifts she took at the Circle K, how many painting students she took on at the community center, she still couldn't scrape enough money together to get to Seattle, pay for school and find a place to live.

As she looked at the bags near the rest of her crew, she knew they'd stolen enough cash by the last job to make them all set. She had more than she needed to get to school and live comfortably while she got her degree. It was her uncle, Hank that pulled her in again. He pushed and bullied her and Danny to do another.

And now, getting an education was way down on her list of things happening anytime soon.

"What do we do, then?" Stan Dodd asked. He was a friend of Hank's from the bars back in New Orleans. "We wait to see if he ever comes back? Sit here and wait for the cops to tear gas us, or start shooting?"

Ricky G nodded. "He's right. It was stupid to put the hostages in the other room. If they figure that out, they'll come in, guns blazing. We're dead."

Lana shook her head. "The hostages were freaking out because of the guard *you* killed. We couldn't keep them so close. Besides…" She turned the monitor around to show them the conference room with all of the customers and employees. "We can watch from here. They aren't going anywhere."

"Doesn't keep us from getting shot."

"Plus, did you really look around outside? There are fewer cops out there than at your average coffee shop," Lana said. "Nobody is rushing us anytime soon."

"Call him." Hank didn't look like he was in the mood to have things explained to him logically.

"Jesus Christ, I did," Lana said. "No answer. No answer the last twelve times you saw me call him." It wasn't like Danny to leave them high and dry with no word on what he was doing. He'd have at least texted her to say he was running, but here, he had gone dark and silent.

"Do it again… Get my asshole nephew back here to pick us up."

Lana stood up and pulled out her cell phone. "Jesus." She looked at the security guard's body as she hit redial on her brother's number. It rang once and then again. Same as it had for the last twenty minutes. Frustrated, she put it on speaker and set it on the counter as it filled the room with the continuous ringing. It never went to voicemail or stopped, just rang on.

"Okay. We get it."

The room went silent again as Stan ended the call.

"What are we going to do?" Ricky G looked more and more uneasy as the minutes dragged on. He briefly looked out the window, stupidly peering out through the pane of broken glass.

"Idiot. Get back or they'd freaking drop you." Hank jerked him by the arm.

"We have to get out of here. I can't stay here anymore."

The silence returned for a moment before the air was filled with sharp cracks and thuds.

3

Eli and Gino turned at the sound of a revving engine and the shrill sound of metal scraping against something. An old Chevy four-door careened out of the parking garage of the hotel across the street, crashing through the barriers police had set up to keep people from wandering into the middle of a shootout, should one erupt.

"The hell?" Gino said. "Somebody stop this guy."

The car swerved and headed directly for the police cars in the street. The driver leaned out of his window and fired several shots from a handgun as he picked up speed.

Several officers turned their attention from the bank to the car suddenly bearing down on them and started shooting back. The car continued to drive crazily, swerving from side to side as it went. The driver stopped shooting and ducked down, guiding his vehicle into the hail of gunfire from the police.

"The heck is this guy thinking?" Eli asked. He ran for the sidewalk on the other side of the street and dove behind a car there. Gino followed, but several officers stayed put and continued to fire until the last possible moment.

The old chevy dodged, fishtailing into one of the patrol cars and sending it sliding across the pavement. In a moment, the car slid to a stop in front of the bank. There, the driver began firing again at the scattered officers.

Almost simultaneously, the bank doors flew open and Eli saw the suspects run out, firing their automatic weapons in all directions as they dashed for the car. The first two out were bigger, with the last one out likely the female Gino mentioned.

As Eli drew his sidearm, a thump drew his attention toward the first man out of the bank as he fell to the ground. The glass of the door behind him shattered and the man behind was suddenly covered in blood. The sniper had maintained her focus on the bank rather than the approaching car.

"The rest of you, stop. You're under arrest," Eli shouted toward the bank. He used the car as cover and trained his gun toward the bank. The rest of the criminals had ducked after the first shot, and had disappeared from his view.

Another thud erupted from the sniper and the back window of the car shattered.

Eli broke cover and moved toward the squad cars and SUV. Three officers were already there as he approached.

"Let's get around to the back of their car and see if we can put a stop to this," Eli said. "You two go low, and I'll stay up and see if I can hit the driver."

Before anyone could acknowledge the plan, the car's tires squealed and the vehicle darted ahead, pulling away from the bank and the police cars.

"Damn it," Eli said. He stepped from cover and fired at the suddenly accelerating car. His shots hit the car and likely somewhere in the interior. The car didn't slow, or waver off course. The deputies with Eli fired as well, but nobody inside was visible. If anyone was hit, the police likely wouldn't know until they caught up with the gang.

More thuds indicated the sniper took a couple of additional tries at stopping the car, with no luck. The car slammed into the front of the city police car blocking the road, spinning it around, but continued to tear off out of town.

Once the car vanished, Eli started running the reasons for their failure through his head, looking at blame, looking at the weakness of their efforts. The unfortunate timing of the accident on the nearby freeway was a huge factor. Deputies and troopers alike were working that pileup, drawing valuable resources away from the bank. The cars and trucks there blocked lanes and diverted traffic, causing a tie-up for miles, which also slowed down other agents and other agencies from helping. Beyond that? It was easy to blame individuals for not being in the correct positions, local law enforcement for not being prepared, and on the bureau itself for not being more vigilant about this particular crew of bank robbers.

In the end, he wanted to say it was no one's fault, even if it was everyone's fault.

No matter what he decided, it didn't get them any closer to the fleeing suspects.

Millet crouched down to examine the broken glass shimmering in the hot Florida morning sun. The sidewalk right outside the bank was covered in it for ten feet or so. "Well, this is a helluva start to the morning for this sleepy town." Eli was pissed there wasn't a car left in working order he could use to help pursue the perps. His car had a flat tire, and one of the squad cars wouldn't start. The SUV was leaking gas and radiator fluid. He imagined the suspects got lucky, because the damage would have taken an expert to cause.

"Right?" Gino looked on grimly from behind Eli.

"Anyone get a look at the plates on the getaway vehicle? Better description of the suspects?"

"Nah, happened too fast. We're waiting on a tag number from the pursuing officers." He turned and pointed across the street. "There's a camera or two on the grocery parking lot over there, and another on the ATM across the street. Hoping to get lucky with those, but we'll check the others in town, just in case. Any one of them might have caught these guys casing the place, or the guy pulling into the garage."

Eli stood and looked through the remnants of the window. Inside the bank he could see the mess of papers and brochures littering the floor. More glass, a briefcase, other items scattered around on the tile floor. His gaze fell to the man slumped against the far wall. "The bank guard?"

"Ted Ruby? Worked part time here at the bank, and part time as a deputy over in Lafayette. Witnesses say he barely got off a shot before the suspects gunned him down. Sounds like there wasn't much he could do."

"Okay. So, they shot a deputy. That makes them a little higher up on our list." Eli felt a little behind, as the local cops and state troopers had already worked the crime scene before he got there. He had a long haul in from the field office in Jacksonville which wasted a good two hours for him. "I wasn't aware of the fact he was on the job. Well, what else can you tell me? We've had a crew robbing banks over in Louisiana near the border, and they sound similar. Well, except the other gang hasn't killed anyone."

"Don't know what to tell you. Sounds like three suspects came in, one female and two males, took what they could. No names were spoken, in fact, they said very little. No accents, no visible tattoos, or hair color. They wore ski masks and sunglasses, so facial features and eye colors are unknown, even. Then shit went sideways when we showed up."

Eli stepped gingerly into the bank, careful not to disturb the scene. The description sure sounded like the suspects he'd been after for the other jobs. In those jobs, witnesses noticed a man waiting for them outside in the getaway car. A different vehicle each time. Man's description varied from a blonde in a ballcap to a brunette with sunglasses. Eli was interested to see if they could get a good description of the driver who pulled this off. This time they might help identify him, or at least see the guy's amusing new disguise on camera.

"We've got the bank cams and we're happy to share the footage, maybe you can get something off of it to help compare to your gang," Gino said. He turned and waved another trooper in. This one was a shorter woman with her blonde hair pulled back in a ponytail threaded through the back of her black ballcap. She wasn't wearing all the tactical gear the others were. "Special agent Eli Millet? This is trooper Dakota Irwin. She was our eye in the sky this morning."

They shook hands and Eli gave her a sideways look. "Some nice work, you been at this for long?"

Dakota nodded. "Yeah, a few years, now. Sorry I couldn't help with the truck or the other suspects."

"You did fine, you got one of them." Gino nodded to where the crime scene techs had already started taking pictures.

"What's his story?" Dakota asked.

Just outside the bank, a couple of techs were examining the body of the downed bank robber. Next to his body was a semiautomatic rifle and an extra clip.

"Him? Not much yet. We're waiting on the coroner," Gino said. "We almost didn't get Dakota's help this morning. She was out chasing down weirdos. What was it this time? They have you chasing Batman?" Gino smiled.

"You're thinking of Mothman. And no. This ended up with a simple Peeping Tom in a Halloween mask."

"But?" Gino asked. "What was the call originally?"

Shaking her head, Dakota reluctantly replied "They called 9-1-1 to say Freddy Kruger from those '*Nightmare*' movies was looking in their window."

Eli couldn't help but chuckle along with the others. "I started out on patrol with the Paducah Kentucky. Believe me, I remember the good old days in uniform, we got the same sort of calls." He led the others outside, doing the same dance to avoid evidence on the carpet.

"You were a trooper?" Dakota asked.

"Nah, local P.D. Back home in Kentucky we used to get some strange ass calls too. Bog beasts, Bigfoot, Frogmen. Zombies. Hell, those were more fun than real cases sometimes, right?"

"If you say so," Gino said.

"Paducah is famous for the National Quilt Museum," Eli said. "Let's say it was a quiet town, most of the time. A little variety made it bearable."

Gino nodded and said, "Look, I have to get on back to the lab and check with the techs on the forensics and head up the command center. Trooper Irwin will work with you and get anything you need. She can take you back to the barracks and get you some office space, and then, we'll loop you in on the progress. We'll loan her out to you for as long as the Bureau needs our assistance." Gino turned and trotted away to a nearby squad car. "Check in with me from time to time, Irwin, okay?" He slammed the door and the car took off.

"Well, I guess we're working together." Eli watched Gino leave in a patrol car round the corner and disappear into the city of Ludlow Crossing.

Dakota sighed and agreed.

"Uh, look, trooper Irwin, I uh… I work really well on my own, so if you can disentangle yourself from this babysitting assignment, you feel free. Drop me at the barracks and get on with your life. I'm fine with it. I mean, the Bureau people should be here soon."

"I think you heard the conversation. They tend to push me at every shit assignment they can find. So, I think we're stuck together."

"I don't think *I'm* a shit assignment, really." Eli laughed. "I guess some people's mileage may vary."

"Look, agent…"

"Eli…"

"Agent Eli, I don't…"

"Just Eli. Call me Eli."

"Okay, Eli. I arrived on site, set up my position, took a shot and here we are. I don't know shit about this robbery other than what I heard on the radio. Not sure how I'm going to be of any help to you."

"You know the area?"

"Sure."

"Feel like going back and sitting in a room looking at paperwork with me?"

"Not particularly."

Millet saw the crime techs around his own vehicle, taking pictures of the bullet holes.

"Can you drive a car?"

"Damn right."

"Do you *have* a car?"

Dakota nodded.

"We'll get along just fine." With that, Eli pulled his bag from the trunk of the dark blue bureau sedan and waited for Dakota to lead the way.

"Seriously?"

"Sure. I need to think. And I think better as a passenger."

They tossed their gear into Dakota's patrol vehicle around the corner of the hotel and got in. "Where are we going?"

"It's your town, I was hoping you'd have an idea." Eli took a sip from his coffee tumbler before placing it in the console. He pointed up the street and Dakota pulled off onto the sleepy city thoroughfare. "On the way up here, I had my people run some info on the bank jobs, locations, personnel, and whatnot. Doing some preliminary comparisons. The crew seems the same as one we've had our eyes on, but this job seems pretty far from the others."

"Not their first job, then?"

"I don't think so. They're roaming a little, if it's them."

The engine revved up a little. "You think they're based over in Louisiana?"

It was Eli's theory in the beginning, now he wasn't so sure. "Maybe they're somewhere closer to the Florida - Louisiana border? I don't know what to think."

"Well, on your drive here, I'm sure you noticed how close this bank is to the highway. Couple streets over and bang, you're off." Dakota stopped at a red light and pointed to the signs nearby indicating interstate ten and highway seventy-one. If you think they're based out of another state, they'd be well on their way before we even got the alarm."

"True." Eli stared at the map rather than the signs around them. "I don't know. Seems like a long way to haul ass back to whatever they're using as a home base back there. If anyone spotted them or they hit a check point or something they'd be fucked," Eli said. "Pardon my language."

"Not a problem." Instead of turning onto the highway, Dakota passed the onramp and drove down a road dotted with fast food restaurants and gas stations. "So, the other option would be to find a place to hide out around here until things died down. Maybe a friend or relative?"

It made sense to Eli, but there wasn't much so far suggesting his suspects had a friend this far away from Louisiana. "Think we'll find anything by driving around for hours?"

"Doubt it."

"Is there anywhere around here with a decent all-day breakfast to go? I didn't get a chance to eat on the way out."

Eli could feel the weight of Dakota's stare. "We just had a shoot-out with multiple robbery suspects and you want to stop for eggs?" She asked.

"I think better on a full stomach? Doesn't have to be anything fancy."

"Whatever you say." Dakota shrugged, "I know plenty of places that definitely aren't anything fancy."

4

Stan shouted from the back seat. "Yes! Fuck you, cops." He punched the seat in front of him, laughing like a school kid.

Curled on the floor of the front passenger seat, Lana covered her ears and held onto the seat as they slammed into the police car and accelerated to a speed she felt in her bones. "Damn it, Danny," she shouted. It was all she could muster, and she was positive he couldn't hear her over the engine, or through his steely look of concentration.

"Jesus, they nailed Ricky G as he came out. He's gone. No way he lived. No way at all." Danny gripped the wheel and scanned his rearview.

"Anyone coming?" Hank asked.

"A couple of squad cars, but they're dodging debris and busted up units. They won't be a problem."

Lana looked up at her brother, worried he might have been shot or injured in the gunfight or somewhere else in the last three minutes the whole escape took. "Dumbass. You should have just gone. You should have run away."

"I'm fine. Stop mothering me. I'm driving."

"Moron. You are supposed to run when we get caught. You could have been shot."

"You could have, too."

Lana knew her brother wasn't wrong, but she couldn't help but apply different rules to him, even if the situations were the same.

As Danny took a sharp corner to point the car down an alley when the engine started knocking loudly.

"Jesus Christ, Danny. What the fuck is wrong with you?" Hank swatted his nephew from the back of the Buick. "This car is a piece of shit."

Lana watched from the passenger seat, worried about her uncle Hank's continued agitation since the bank robbery. His mood had only soured more when the car started making a knocking noise ten minutes after they traded it for their damaged getaway car.

"I didn't have a lot of options in the parking garage. The cops were all around the one I'd picked out for the job in the first place. That was a killer car. And this one seemed fine when I took it," Danny said.

Hank pounded the car door. "Well, it doesn't sound fine now, does it?"

The ailing vehicle crawled along in the alley, its pathetic squeals echoing off the buildings around it in the morning silence. They'd made it to more of a warehouse district north of town before the problem began.

Looking for any way to diffuse the situation, Lana pointed to a gas station sign high above the street up ahead. "Look, we can stop there."

"And what?" Stan had been silent in the back seat next to Hank. "Ask a nice mechanic to fix our car so we can continue our getaway?" Stan worried Lana. Everyone else in the car at this point was family, but Stan was only a friend of Hanks. Lana and Danny hadn't met him until a few months ago when they started planning the robberies. He was supposedly a former Army Ranger, but Lana thought it was bullshit. It was some story he pulled out of his ass whenever he wanted to be in charge of something.

The car slowed and Lana could hear the tick of the turn signal.

"She's right. This station is a garage, too. I'd bet there's a few cars in good shape. We can boost one of those."

"Brilliant, asshole. If they're there to be fixed, it means there's something wrong with them." Hank looked as if he might smack Danny again.

As Danny brought the car to a halt in front of the pumps, Lana spoke up, "If cars are getting fixed, then there has to be an employee fixing them, right? We'll grab a mechanic's car or something."

Stan and Hank exchanged a glance, before Stan spoke up. "Fine. You get out and fill the gas tank. We need to be prepared to leave if things go sour or we can't find another car." He pointed to Lana. "Got it? And the Boy Wonder here can go scam us some working transportation."

"And the two of us will distract anyone inside and grab some food," Hank said.

"What about cameras?" Lana asked. "No point in leaving your faces out there for all to see."

"We'll handle it," Stan said. Phrases like that were usually code indicating he had no clue what he was doing, at least in Lana's experience.

The group split up, with Danny hanging back until the other two men were inside, and then he began to casually roam through the parking lot near the garage before disappearing around the corner of the filthy building.

Lana pulled the squeegee out of the filthy water and ran it across the back window of the shitty blue car. She knew Danny was careful when he stole it, and even did a thorough check of it before the job. Whatever caused the knocking and the sudden overheating had to be something he couldn't see coming.

She dipped the squeegee back in the sludge and started wiping the front window absently. Her brother hadn't emerged from the corner, and she didn't hear any vehicles starting from over there. In the convenience station, she could see her uncle and Stan wandering around, opening the cooler doors, picking up bags of chips, gathering drinks, and leafing through magazines. The man at the cash register watched them carefully, only glancing once or twice out at Lana. She looked around, taking in the wide stretch of road. There were other gas stations not far off with tall signs and neon prices to attract vehicles from the highway. Cars drifted through fast food drive-throughs, and somewhere in the distance the sounds of construction boomed. The noise lulled her into a stupor as she waited for the gas to finish filling their vehicle. She wondered how she managed to get herself into her current situation. Maybe it was the fear of disappointing her brother or her uncle.

Things happened quickly for her then. Lana had let her guard down and was startled by the triple pops from a pistol. She ducked behind their car, and peered through the windows to see Hank pointing his gun in the direction of the cash register. The clerk and Stan weren't visible, but another shot cracked from somewhere, this one deeper and longer. Lana watched in shock as Hank fell to the ground suddenly.

The squeal of a vehicle turning brought Lana's attention back to the other corner of the building, where a double-cab pickup came roaring toward her with Danny behind the wheel.

"Let's go," Danny said.

Lana grabbed what little supplies they had and tossed them into the back of the vehicle as more shots echoed in the store, shattering one of the plate glass windows. She didn't notice Danny was already at her side, grabbing the duffle bags they'd stuffed with cash from the robbery. He tossed them in the rear of the truck and stepped toward the store before Lana had the peace of mind to grab his arm.

"Don't go in there." Her words stopped Danny and he turned with conflicted wide eyes. "Get back in the car and get ready to drive."

After a half dozen steps toward the store, Stan burst through the door, half-dragging Hank at his side. Blood covered Hank's shirt.

"Open the door, let's go," Stan shouted.

Without asking a question, or reacting to the scene in front of her, Lana turned and bounded to their new ride, swinging the rear passenger door open for the men and then climbing into the front passenger seat.

"Is the money in here?" Stan shoved Hank inside and slammed the door before running around to the other side and stepping in.

"Do you think we'd go through this and forget it?" Lana thought it was a dumb, heat of the moment question, but it was stupid nonetheless.

"Then go," Hank said. "Get out of here."

Everyone jerked back in their seats as Danny floored the gas and they pulled out onto the nearly empty road. He managed to toe a line between reckless and average driver somehow as he moved them further into the swamplands.

"What happened?" Danny asked.

Hank groaned.

"The clerk got twitchy. I had no choice." Stan sounded angry. More at having to answer the question, than at what happened.

"Do we have anything to stop the bleeding in here?" Hank moaned again.

"I don't know, this isn't our car." Lana opened the glovebox and started digging through the papers and wrappers, tossing them on the floor. "Electrical tape?"

"Hand me that," Stan said. "I can use his shirt to stop the blood and tape it on to keep the pressure steady." He went to work, doing as he said. Lana wondered if maybe his military stories were true and he'd picked up something in first aid training.

"What happened to the clerk?" Danny asked.

Stan continued to work on Hank, staring at the tape as he wrapped it.

"Hello? What happened to the clerk?"

5

It took about twenty minutes for someone to come upon the gas station with the dead clerk. After that, the law enforcement circus showed up almost immediately, including Eli and Dakota. They were not too far away when the call came in, having stopped at a diner called Linda Lee's House of Hotcakes. Eli had to admit Dakota was spot on about her breakfast choice. Within a couple of minutes of ordering they had two bags of amazing smelling food, which they'd barely broken into when the call came in about the convenience store fight.

"Anyone get a look at which way they went?" Eli asked the officer interviewing witnesses.

"Nah. These people got here way after the action," the woman said. "We have a couple of officers canvassing the restaurants and other businesses in both directions, hopefully they'll find a witness or some surveillance footage."

"This their getaway car?" Eli pointed to the crappy Buick by the pumps.

"From what we can figure. We're checking to figure out if they stole a car from the garage, or a customer, or what."

"Any cameras in the shop?"

The officer shook her head and said, "There's a camera inside, but it doesn't seem to be working."

With a nod, Eli stepped back to Dakota. "Well, they only could have gone one of two ways."

"You want to flat-out guess which way they went?"

Eli shrugged. "Why not? Did they turn around and go back the way they came, hoping no one would recognize them in a new car, or head away from the city?"

Eli watched as Dakota laughed and looked up and down the stretch of road. "Suppose they could've headed back and got on the highway before we were even aware of what happened here. They could've driven right past every officer and squad car in whatever vehicle they stole without us even knowing."

"Huh. So, you think they headed back into town?"

"You don't?"

Eli shrugged. "No clue. Just asking." He wasn't trying to mess with her, but she second guessed nearly everything she said to him. "What was that business back at the bank with Gino talking about some monsters or something? What was he saying?"

"You said you'd had those crank calls before."

"Yeah, but it sounded like something more than a crank."

"Fine. We'll go north, away from Ludlow Crossing." Looking more than a little angry, Dakota walked toward the squad car. "Let's go."

"Yes, ma'am." Eli guessed she really didn't want to talk about the dumb calls she had to respond to out in the middle of nowhere.

They both got into the vehicle, but before they could leave, another deputy approached, waving his arms. He leaned down to Eli's open window and said "The mechanic in the back didn't make it."

"Okay." Eli knew that changed things a bit. Two dead at the gas station now, added to the dead guard at the bank.

"We checked with the hospital and we searched the garage, but so far we haven't found his keys. One of the other employees says he drove one of those big pickup trucks with the extra row of seats. All we have right now for a color is light green. Might help as you search. We'll see if we can get more information." The deputy waved and headed back to the garage as the squad car turned and pulled out onto the four-lane stretch of road.

"A green pickup? Really doesn't narrow it down around here," Dakota said. "It's like saying to watch out for a jet at the airport."

"It might help," Eli looked out the window, staring at each business, restaurant and warehouse for a double cab truck. "You don't seem to have too much faith in the description, though."

"You see more trucks than any other vehicle around here. We'll be turning our heads like they're on a swivel as we drive through town. Liable to get whiplash."

"They don't have trucks where you come from?"

"Not this many."

"And where is this paradise?"

Dakota sighed. "I was in the NAVY, with Special Operations Command. Did time with hostage rescue and recovery. A few other posts. MacDill AFB in Florida wasn't so bad."

"Wow. And you ended up here in the panhandle as a cop. Sounds like a good skill set for law enforcement. How come you weren't a lifer? What made you get out of the military?"

"You are full of questions, aren't you?" Dakota asked.

With a shrug, Eli said, "The only way you get answers, right? Besides, it feels like we're becoming fast friends." Eli laughed. So far, the trooper's demeanor was anything but excited to work with him.

Dakota didn't crack a smile. "To your earlier question: There's an elderly woman out in the swamp, name's Ramona. She lives off of semi-legal trapping out in the swamps. Has traps all over the region."

"Yeah?"

"Well, she catches gators, fishes for swamp bass, all sorts of things. If it lives out there, she's caught it at least once or twice. Whatever makes her money, you know?"

Eli knew a lot of illegal trappers growing up, but they were mostly after things on the land and in the woods, like coyotes and bobcats. He didn't know anyone who'd deliberately gone after prehistoric monsters like alligators. Seemed like a good way to lose some important body parts.

"So, Ramona sometimes has some… unique complaints. She's reported flying saucers out over her home on more than one occasion. Flew right over her house, she swears."

"Little green men try to abduct her, I think they may be in for a fight," Eli said, thinking about an old lady who traps alligators for a living.

"She's never actually suggested seeing any aliens, though. Not once."

Eli laughed. "And you aren't worried about an invasion from space?"

"Well, she does live fairly close to Eglin and Hurlburt Field Air Force Bases. Her home is right outside their respective flight paths," Dakota's eyebrows raised slightly. "So, we figure maybe those things are connected."

"And the skunk monster he mentioned?"

"Skunk *ape*," Dakota corrected. "You have to get it right around these parts."

"My apologies."

"The skunk ape is a local legend. Kind of the Sunshine State's version of bigfoot. Only our Sasquatch smells like a sewer."

"Go Florida."

"Yay for us. Beyond being smelly, this thing is skinnier than your typical description of a bigfoot, maybe a little shorter. They build nests or something out in the swamps, apparently keep to themselves, and occasionally harass people for food and whatnot."

"And the old woman has met one?"

"Oh, sure. And they've stolen her fish and crabs and whatnot from her traps."

"Seriously? That's a thing out here? Wandering into the marshes to abscond with the daily catch?"

The deputy's answer was interrupted by a call for her on the radio.

"Patrol three, proceed to thirty-one Kenwood Drive. See the complainant near your location about a ten-fifty-seven with PD. Description matches missing vehicle in convenience store shooting and bank robbery."

Eli grabbed the mic and keyed it in. "Patrol three, copy. Show us ten-seventy-six." A hit and run would sound like a dead end to him normally, but their suspects were in a hurry and not likely to stop and trade insurance information with someone if they dinged their bumper.

"We're not far. Couple of minutes, tops." In the driver's seat, Dakota accelerated the vehicle quickly, pushing Eli back in his seat. He knew to trust the trooper and her training, but he still grabbed the armrest of his seat and held on. She took corners without slowing numerous times and he could feel his fingers digging into the plastic of the door. Still, he did his best to hold a smile on his face.

Halfway up Kenwood Drive, Dakota slowed for a waving woman standing by a rusting Chevelle with a long scrape down the driver's side of the vehicle.

"That was fast," the woman said. "Idiots just hit me."

Eli didn't finish getting out of the patrol car. "Yeah? How long ago?"

The barefoot woman shook her head, "I don't know. Like, maybe ten minutes ago? Maybe less?"

"No shit?" Eli asked. "Which way did they go?" He slid back into his seat and kept the door open long enough to hear the woman's reply.

"Down there, and then they turned right at the intersection." She pointed toward the stop sign in the distance.

As the car accelerated, Eli rolled the window down and shouted his thanks.

6

More trees whipped by as Lana looked out the window of the truck. The right rearview mirror was gone from when they'd sideswiped the car and almost hit the woman next to it. They'd been driving at an insane pace for almost an hour since the gas station fiasco. Hank had quieted down after a half hour, the adrenaline of the incident wearing off and his anger abating. Eventually, Stan had declared the wound wasn't nearly as bad as it could have been. He'd used some rags to stem the bleeding and get a better look at the injury.

"Where the hell are we going?" Danny sounded tense, his voice was calm and subdued. Lana assumed he was trying to keep the peace between the front and back seats. He'd followed directions from Hank up to that point, but Hank seemed less sure of himself.

"We're looking for a turnoff after a small marina," Hank moaned. You can't miss it."

"Marina? In the swamp?" Lana asked. They were far enough north; any kind of building was rare. They'd headed into the marshes of a protected forest and water management area. Following Black Creek Road was a dangerous proposition. If something else went wrong, if there was flooding somewhere, they had no choice other than to turn around and go back the way they came. And it would likely mean driving into what had to be a widening net of law enforcement.

"There's some place where they give tourists rides on airboats, or they leave for fishing trips. It's perfect. We'll grab a boat and find this old house and hole up a bit." Stan sounded like a weight was lifting, as if he could see the light at the end of the tunnel.

Danny slowed, his head turning from side to side. "I don't see no damn turn, no marina, no fucking fishing boats."

The trees thickened overhead, blotting out the afternoon Florida sun. The canopy of leaves and branches made the stretch ahead look like a railroad tunnel, dark and forbidding. Lana peered into the crisscross of foliage alongside them, searching for a turnoff or a marina. Ahead, the light reminded her of a train coming from the opposite end of the tunnel. If there was a business, a boat dock, or another living soul out in those thick trees, she couldn't see it.

"Shit." The truck swerved and Danny cursed some more. As the sound of the brakes rose to a squeal, Lana heard a thud on the side of the vehicle seconds before it shuddered to a stop.

"What the fuck?" Stan shouted. His sentiment was echoed by nearly everyone else. "What are you doing?"

"Did you not see that shit?"

"What?" Lana asked. "I didn't see anything." Her eyes had been scanning the trees on the right for any sign of an overgrown turnoff.

Danny seemed more panicked than Lana had seen him. "I don't know, it might have been a kid," Danny said. "It ran out in front of us. Oh, shit."

"Just go." Stan didn't sound the least bit concerned. "We can't sit here."

Lana held up her hands to calm the men in the back seat. "Chill the fuck out," she said. "Let me look and see. It's dark in the shadows, I'm sure it's an animal, like a possum or something." She opened her door and grabbed the pistol from between her and her brother.

Danny grabbed her wrist and said, "Lana, it wasn't any damn possum."

"It's okay." She nodded to reassure her brother she believed him. "Be right back."

"You better be quick, girl," Hank grunted from the back seat.

Lana ignored him, tired of his bluster and his implied threats already.

The gravel and weeds crunched below her as her feet hit the torn-up pavement. She gripped the gun tighter, suddenly aware of the shadows and shapes around her in the light that made it through the trees. She stepped toward the front of the vehicle, but stopped quickly, hit by a horrible stench suddenly. She recoiled, nearly nauseated by the smell like manure and sulfur.

"Ugh," she groaned, trying to cover her nose with her shirt with one hand, while still gripping the pistol. "The fuck is that smell?"

"What is it?" Danny shouted from the vehicle, straining to see out the window.

Doing her best to ignore the stench, she held up a hand to get Danny to wait a minute more as she walked to the front of the truck. The smell was stronger there, and she covered her nose with her arm.

Slowly, cautiously, she crouched down to look under the truck. There was a small dent in the fender and the dark red splatter of blood. She followed it around to the side and found more of it dripping onto the ground. She figured it was fresh or it would've been dry by then. Lana followed the sticky line of dark, sticky back toward the rear of the vehicle, where the trail ended both on the vehicle and on the ground.

She scanned the gravelly road behind them and noticed a dark shape in the grass, hidden among the shadows.

"Let's fucking go," Stan said. "It's nothing."

Lana ignored him and walked carefully toward the lump in the shade of the trees about fifty yards behind them. It was small, just as Danny had said, and it wasn't moving. On the ground, she noticed a few fresh splatters of blood.

The weeds were tall along the side of the road, combining with the trees to block out much of the Florida sunshine. She heard weeds snap nearby and paused to listen for it again. She had no idea what was wandering around in those particular marshes. She knew alligators were common, but she'd heard about huge snakes and other animals lurking in the water *and* out of it. She stood still for almost a minute before she decided she'd only startled herself with things that weren't there.

She got to the crumpled form at the side of the road and, though she was standing directly over it, she still had no idea what she was looking at.

"What is it? It ain't a kid, is it?" Danny leaned out his window, looking worried as Lana had ever seen him.

"No." She didn't sound too sure, not even to herself. What lay below her was maybe four feet tall, thin and wiry, covered in muddy, matted hair. If she didn't know better, she'd swear it was some kind of monkey. But the idea of a monkey roaming the swamps seemed more ridiculous to her than just about anything in the moment. And it was such an odd shape for a monkey. So skinny, with long thin legs and arms.

She hesitated to check to see if it was dead. Something about the smell made her want to keep her distance. Looking at it, she could make out a huge cut on its rounded head. That seemed to be where the majority of the bleeding had occurred, though she could tell one of the legs was at an unnatural angle and more cuts crisscrossed its chest.

Behind her, the truck door slammed and Hank made his way toward her angrily. "The hell is taking so long? You saying a prayer for a dearly departed squirrel or some shit? In case you forgot, we need to keep moving."

"I'm aware."

"What the fuck is that smell?" He asked. His gaze fell to the thing in the grass and his expression turned sour. "Is it a…" Lana could see he was puzzling something out by the confused look on his face."

"I don't know what it is."

"It's a… a… lemur." He sounded confident in his assertion.

"It's not a lemur."

"I watch the fucking Animal Channel all the time. It's a lemur."

"There's no tail. Jesus, it's not a lemur."

The weeds across the road rustled and both Hank and Lana turned abruptly to see what would emerge.

When the sound stopped and nothing emerged, Hank laughed and pointed at Lana. "Shit, girl. You shoulda seen your face. You looked like you were going to piss yourself."

"You're an asshole."

"Whatever, let's go. It's a dead lemur." Hank walked back toward the door to the truck. Halfway there, the tall weeds closest to him started rustling. "What now, a terrifying squirrel?" He laughed and grabbed the truck's handle.

Lana stared at the thing for a few more seconds, and none of them changed her mind: It wasn't a damn lemur, no matter what the resident Nature Channel expert said. The bloody, dead thing made her shiver. Whatever it actually was, it made her want to turn around and make her way out of the marsh and never come back.

Behind her, the door to the truck slammed and she realized she was alone. The only thing that kept her from running back to the vehicle herself was the fact she had the pistol in her hand. It made her feel a fraction of an inch safer. Plus, she didn't want to give Hank the satisfaction of seeing her afraid.

"The hell was it?" Danny asked. "Hank keeps saying it was a lemur."

Shaking her head, Lana said, "I still think it was too big for those things. But whatever it was, it's dead now. No reason to argue about it, I guess."

As her brother got the truck moving again, Lana stared into the side mirror, trying to get a glimpse of the lump in the road behind them, and while she hoped to get a look at another one emerging from the weeds, she was disappointed. Nothing new appeared.

Ahead the road narrowed, and got closer to the water on the right. There really was no turn back here, marsh on the right, thick trees on the left and little to no shoulder on either side. Lana looked out on the water, seeing little but shore birds in flight.

As the road began to widen a bit again, Stan shifted and pointed at an object ahead. "What's that over there? Is it a marina?"

Danny shook his head. "No. Jesus. It's just a dude with a fishing boat and some nets or something."

"Stop, then," Hank said. "Stop."

"Why?" Danny asked, as he slowed the vehicle a little.

"Just do it," Stan said.

Lana sighed, wondering what the new plan would be and why they couldn't stick to the original idea of finding the house out in the marshes and hiding there. Her uncle was headstrong and made snap decisions dragging them further from their goal.

"Take the boat, we'll get there faster than this."

"What about the kid with it?" Stan asked, pulling his gun out.

"Bring him for now. Maybe he can get us there faster," Hank said. "We can ditch him later."

Lana had an idea of what he meant by 'ditch him later' and she shuddered a little at the idea of another death because of their actions. All of the other robberies had gone smoothly and bloodlessly. As Stan hid his pistol in his belt, Lana slid her uncle's gun into her hand and held it behind her back, following Stan out of the car and toward the figure by the boat, tending to nets and traps.

"Hey," Hank muttered. "Get back here." But there was no way for him to stop her. She'd made it out, not closing the door and was already walking casually, ten or so paces behind Stan.

The figure with the boat was a young man with a patchy beard and an old, faded brown baseball cap on his head. His arms and legs were dark brown, tanned by the Florida sun. He was pulling fish out of a net when Stan got to him, but he never looked up.

"Hey," Stan said. The young man didn't turn around or acknowledge the presence of two new people in his midst. Stan quickly lifted his foot and shoved the kid over with one push of his muddy boot. In the next moment, the young man was on his ass, headphones on the ground next to him with rock music blaring from them. His wide eyes told Lana he was shocked to have strangers interrupting his work. Around him, soaking wet nets and wire framed traps dried in the Florida sunlight.

"I asked if that was your boat," Stan said. "You stupid or something?"

"I didn't hear you is all."

"You hear me now, right? Can you operate this thing or not?" Stan was tapping his pistol against his side, which Lana assumed wasn't helping the kid answer. "You know what buttons to push, all that shit?"

"Yeah, but it ain't my boat. Shit, I couldn't ever buy one of those."

Lana knew nothing about boats, but she could still see this one was a piece of shit. It was big enough for maybe six people, but it smelled of dead fish and whatever the hell they'd been using for bait. Scuffed, dinged and patched in places, she was slightly surprised it floated. The words 'Marsh Mellow' were hand-painted on the side. For the kid to be in awe of it, surely said something about his economic situation. "Look, Stan, we can find another one somewhere up the road. This is a little worse for wear."

"Nah, this is perfect. This'll work." Stan turned and waved his hand at the others in the truck, motioning for them to come over. Lana ran to help her uncle get out and carry some money. "Get this thing started, dude."

The young man looked at him dumbly. "What? I can't do that. I'm responsible for this. If I'm not here when my boss gets back, I'm in big trouble. This boat is her *baby*. This is her *Marsh Mellow*."

Lana could hear him all the way from the truck and she wondered if the kid understood the danger he was currently in. If it registered with this kid how on edge Stan was. She only hoped he wouldn't do something drastic while she was gone and couldn't stop him. It was debatable if she could do anything to Stop Stan short of killing him. There was no way she'd overpower him, and she had no Jedi mind tricks to talk him out of his crazy thoughts at this point.

"What's your name kid?" Danny asked as he got closer.

"I'm Ollie."

"Well, Ollie, let's get on the same page here. We are not fucking around and we need you to help us now. If you do what we say, you'll be able to get this boat back in one piece. If we have to take it from you, odds are good we'll damage it but good."

Stan leaned in and pulled the hammer of his pistol. "Get the fuck in and get this thing going."

It looked to Lana like the kid might actually say no and get himself shot, but after a few thoughts, he dropped his nets and waded into the water. Mumbling a few choice words, he climbed the ladder and started the engine. She was relieved there wasn't going to be more bloodshed. There was enough already, and things can only get worse.

Stan helped Hank aboard and Lana followed. The swamp water didn't look at all inviting to Lana, but she stepped in anyway, sinking almost to her knees in the muck. Even with the ladder to grip, she found she couldn't pull her leg free. She tugged and yanked her best, but it was stuck fast. She turned to tell Danny, but she was interrupted.

Across the road, an old woman emerged and shouted to the group. "What the hell you doing in my boat?" Her voice was gravelly and deep. "Get the fuck out."

"Shit," Hank shouted.

"That's my boss," Ollie said. He pointed at the angry woman advancing on them. "Told you she wouldn't be happy."

The woman raised a double-barreled shotgun and fired it into the air. "I said get the fuck out of there." She moved faster toward the group, her gun now aimed at them, rather than the sky.

"Danny, help me, I'm stuck," Lana shouted to her brother. She'd tugged with all the strength she could to get her foot free, but the mud and muck held her fast. She heard the splash of her sibling jumping into the water at almost the same time as she heard another blast of the shotgun.

"Shit," Hank shouted. "Let's go."

The motor on the boat glubbed to life, filling the air with thick black smoke. Someone on the boat fired two shots at the old lady, which brought a stream of curse words from her.

Danny sloshed over to Lana and grabbed her knee. "Come on. Let's get you out of here."

"My thoughts exactly."

"On the count of three, let's both pull, okay?" Danny's grip hurt as he tightened his hands around her leg.

She nodded and they counted together up to three and pulled. More gunfire erupted from both directions above them, spurring them on. With a loud slurping sound, they managed to get her out, causing them both to fall back into the dark water. One after another, they climbed the short ladder, tossing themselves into the boat. Hank again shouted for the kid to move the boat before leaning over and shooting at the old woman in the road.

The engine suddenly sputtered, sounding more like a lawnmower than a boat. The whole craft shuddered before taking off at a more acceptable speed, bouncing on the light waves and tearing through the tall swamp grass.

The kid waved at the old woman and shouted "I'm sorry."

7

Eli and Dakota sped toward the area the dispatcher indicated, taking narrow gravel roads connected to obscure grass-covered dirt trails, and finally up onto a poorly-paved drive which flattened out and gave them a slightly smoother ride. Eli admired how well Dakota knew the area, able to turn without second guessing her sense of direction, and without losing speed. However, he was staring at the suddenly evaporating bars on his phone signal when she suddenly stopped.

"Are we there?"

Pointing up ahead, Dakota said, "No, I didn't want to hit whatever's up ahead."

In the shade of the trees lining either side of the road, a trio of shapes were making their way slowly from one grassy ditch to the other. The darkness of the shade hid the details, but to Eli, it looked like three teenagers loping along in the Florida afternoon. Except, something was off. There was something about them that set his senses on alert.

"Those aren't kids, are they?" He asked.

It took a second but Dakota answered, "I don't think so."

Impulsively, Eli opened his door and planted his foot to get out.

"Are you stupid? Look at those things."

The trio stopped in the road and turned toward the car, investigating just as Eli was.

"Eli, wait." The squad car's lights clicked on and illuminated the path, revealing the three were not lanky teens, but thin, hairy creatures. Their arms flew up to shade their gleaming red eyes as they shrank back from the light. In a second, they bounded from their positions and into the trees and weeds, chirping and whooping as they vanished from the road.

"The hell?" Eli couldn't stop himself from stepping completely out of the vehicle and walking toward the spot where the things had been. As he went, he looked back at Dakota, trying to make sure she'd seen the same thing. She hadn't left her seat, and stared at him with wide eyes.

There was nothing indicating the things had ever been there. The asphalt was thick here and clean of any sand or dirt that might have captured a footprint. He wandered around until he noticed a good-sized pool of something up ahead. He leaned close to it and after testing it, was pretty sure it was blood.

"What do you have?" Dakota's door was open and she leaned against it, half in the car and half out.

"Looks like blood, but it's started to dry, so it probably isn't from whatever the hell those things were." He thought for a moment that it could be related to the bank robbery, but it was far too soon to tell. "What the hell were those things?" He looked at Dakota, but held little hope she could be definitive about it.

"I've made a lot of runs out here to answer some weird call or another," Dakota said. "Maybe some of them weren't crackpots. Maybe they've actually seen something."

It wasn't what Eli wanted to hear, but he had nothing else. "So, what? Those were aliens or…"

"I was thinking they were skunk apes. You know, Florida's nasty smelling bigfoot cousins?"

He felt a pain behind his eyes that usually signaled a migraine. "I don't know."

As they stared off at the weeds nearby, they were startled by screeching sound not far away. It was enough of a scare Eli grabbed for his pistol, but he stopped short of pulling it.

"Sounds like metal scraping on something," Dakota said. "Maybe it's the witness we're supposed to meet?"

Eli looked around one more time, struggling not to go stomping into the brush to see what the things were. "Yeah. Fine." He quickly returned to the vehicle and got in. "Skunk ape, huh?"

"We can talk about it later, let's focus on the task at hand. Woman who called us is named Ramona." She pulled ahead and after barely a minute, they noticed the missing pickup truck parked in the grass with all its doors open not far from the thick trees where they'd been. There was also a mess of tangled fishing netting, and an old woman tugging at a rowboat on the opposite side of the road. As he and Dakota pulled up, they got an earful from her.

"About damn time," Ramona said. "Now help me carry this damn boat across the road."

Seeing a skinny old woman attempt to drag a boat up an embankment and onto the pavement wasn't something Eli had on his bingo card that day. "Look. Ma'am. Can we stop a minute and have you go through your story for us?" He noticed Dakota inspecting the truck behind him.

"We don't have time for this. You two meandered up here slow enough, now they have at least an hour head start on us. Maybe more." She tugged harder on the bow of the boat. "Now get your hands on the other end of this thing and let's get a move on."

Eli couldn't believe what she was saying. "Look, we're not going after them in your little row boat."

"You plan on walking through the swamp? Good luck. Besides," Ramona said. "There's a small motor under the tarp by the seat. You drop it in the water and away we go. Slicker than shit."

"There's blood in the back seat. Decent amount of it, too." Dakota approached from the truck.

"Guess the store clerk got someone during the robbery," Eli said. He turned back to Ramona. "Look. This is a big deal now. These people have killed two people at a service station and another at the bank. We need to hear what happened so we can get helicopters and boats and everything else out in this swamp."

The woman sighed and let go of the boat. Eli could see the anger in her eyes, but wasn't entirely sure it was aimed at him. "Okay. I was fishing out on this here boat. I was finishing up when I heard shouting and I came up and saw these people pushing my employee around and trying to steal my other boat. So..." Ramona leaned into the small craft and pulled a shotgun out. "I pulled out Old Smoke here and gave them a few warning shots." She waved the gun around in the air randomly.

"Whoa," Eli said as he and Dakota ducked. "Whoa. Easy, there. Can you just not do that? Is the gun loaded?"

"Of course, it's loaded. What am I, stupid? What if those assholes come back?"

"Fine, but can you set it down for us Ramona?" Dakota looked much calmer than Eli felt. He wondered if maybe she was used to the crazy lady waving a gun, because it didn't seem to faze her.

"I'll put it back in the boat, so it's ready when we catch these people. That way, I can put a few holes in their asses for messing with Ollie."

"Ollie is your employee?" Eli asked.

"Yeah. Known him since he was a boy. He's helped clear my traps since he was knee high to a gator's eye. If these people hurt him…" Ramona trailed off. "Help me move the damn boat."

"Look, I know Ollie means a lot to you. I met him once when I was out here to talk to you. He's a nice young man, Ramona. But we have to get the right people in here to help us do this, and that means not putting you at risk. You need to let us do our jobs," Dakota said.

Ramona dropped the boat and stared hard at Dakota. Eli worried the woman might actually be crazy enough to try to fight the trooper to get her to help get the small craft into the water. Instead, she locked her arms at her sides and looked Dakota up and down for a few seconds. "Look. You're here to catch these guys? I want the same thing. But," The woman paused, taking deep breaths, still staring at Dakota. "The difference between you and me is I know all the places they might go. I know how to get there, and I can take you there to get this thing over with quickly. You two? You'll have to call people, you'll have to wait, you have to explain." She waved her arms around. "Blah, blah, blah. My Ollie could be dead by then, my boat sunk, my life ruined."

"Look," Eli started.

"No. They could run before your people get here. Let's go."

They walked away from Ramona and looked at the truck again as they talked.

"She's right. I mean, it could take a while to get a crew back here to help. We can call now and give them these coordinates. At least get them here," Eli said. "We can give them updates as we go." They'd be better off waiting, since they had no idea how many people were waiting at the suspect's hideout. Maybe they had backup joining them on the run.

"We can, but I have to warn you, the cell and radio service is pretty bad out here. It's hard to say if we'll get in contact again," Dakota replied.

"Fine, radio it in, and I'll see what I can do about this boat."

"We taking Ramona?"

Eli sighed. "Not sure if we have a choice really, not if we want to go *right now*."

8

Danny's driving had given Lana a bruising from the speed and the hard turns, but his skills with a boat were absolutely making her sick.

"Where are we going?" Ollie asked.

"That's what you need to help us with," Hank said. "We're looking for the way across the swamp and up into these cabins near Taylor Creek. Get us close and you're free to go home."

"What?" Ollie looked confused. "You mean like, the Hideaway Hills and the Marshview rentals?"

Hank shrugged. "Yeah, I guess that's the area."

"Where do you think you are?" Ollie asked. "Those are a couple of hours north east of here. Maybe more. We'd have to navigate through the swamp, get out of the water about a half hour from here, cross a road, get back in a boat and then keep going for the rest of the way. And I'm honestly guessing here. I've never done it. It's much easier to drive on the back roads."

"Are you shitting me?" Hank asked. "We mapped this out. You're full of crap, kid."

Ollie dug through a compartment next to Danny, and pulled out a well-worn map. "Let me show you. We're way down here, and there's a shitload of rental properties, cabins and campgrounds right around here."

Lana followed the kid's fingers as they traced a line from their current position to the grouping of lodges where they needed to end up. It was a good distance to travel through the swamp with an injured man and a hostage. She also realized that in Ollie's long list of obstacles, he failed to mention it would be dark soon. It was getting late and the sun would fade within the hour.

"You're shitting me. This was your plan? This was how we were escaping?" Lana shouted. "How the hell did you think this would work?"

Hank pushed his way closer to the map, nudging Ollie roughly out of the way. "Here. This isn't my fault, look." He pointed one stained finger at a point closer to the cabins. "We were supposed to get a boat here. Not back there. If we'd managed to do that, we could've taken the boat for a few minutes and been right where we needed to be. It's Danny's damn fault."

"It was your idea to take *this* boat. This is *your* fault." Danny shouted from the wheel of the craft.

Lana stepped between them and got closer to Ollie. "Look, this thing can get us to the cabins, right? There has to be some way."

"No, no way. I was low on gas when you got to me, there's no way to get all the way up there. Not physically, and not with the fuel we have. I'm sorry. It just won't happen."

The men continued to argue, growing louder with Ollie's declaration.

Lana took a breath to clear her head. They couldn't go back. There were likely police and other law enforcement converging on their truck already. "Where can this thing get us?" She asked. "What's around here that could be safe for us, even for the night? A shack, a hunter's lodge, anything." She stared at Ollie and tried to look kind and not at all desperate.

Ollie pointed to the map. "I mean, you can see there's nothing around here."

"Come on, Ollie. You know this place. You know the swamps, right? There has to be some place not on the map. Someplace only the locals know?" Lana didn't really think she was turning on any womanly charm or anything, but she figured the kid was still young enough to fall for flattery.

"Well, the only places I know off hand are some small hunter's stands. Those aren't very big. I guess there's Ramona's house out in the marshes. It's pretty small, but you could all fit pretty easily."

Lana liked the sound of an actual house over sleeping in a hunter's perch or, worse, on the boat itself. But, if Ramona was the woman shooting at them when they took the boat, her place might be the first place anyone looks.

"And?" Hank asked. "Come on. There's gotta be some other places." He pushed Ollie and then grabbed him by the shirt.

If Lana had been trying to finesse the kid, Hank had blown that out of the sky with his bluster. But it looked like the sudden change in tactics worked.

"I mean, there's an old mansion out there on a partially sunken little island. Got swallowed up by nature a long time ago. It's not the best. Not if you want a *nice* place to rest. I heard it's really falling apart, but it could be safe enough to hide out in, I suppose."

"Ever been there?" Lana asked.

"No."

"But you can get us there, right?" Danny chimed in on the conversation.

Ollie nodded. "Yeah. I can show you how to get there. But I can't promise you'll like the place."

9

It wasn't what Eli would've considered luxury transportation, but he knew the old adage about beggars and choosers. The rusty fishing boat sputtered and smoked, but it still managed to keep a steady speed through the shallow waters of the marsh. It was just big enough to hold the three of them without threatening to sink or capsize.

The sun had disappeared behind the trees not long ago, and now the last of the sunlight was threatening to die out as well. Still, Ramona guided the boat as if she had an internal GPS, turning at various patches of reeds and trees, somehow never moving her head more than a degree or two to see what was on her right or left. Eli could still see the concern and anger in the stoic face as they continued with no sign of her friend.

"How much further?" Eli shouted over the roar of the outboard motor.

Ramona pointed off ahead of them.

Eli and Dakota both leaned cautiously forward, squinting into the distance. Eli saw nothing but swampland and water ahead of them. He was about to ask her again, when he noticed a faint light that appeared and disappeared as the leaves swayed in the gentle breeze. As they approached, the source of the light became more apparent. A shack made up of scraps and tarps stood on stilts to keep it high out of the water. The lights appeared to be Christmas tree lights of various colors strung haphazardly across the wall. From inside one window, the slightly brighter light of a bare bulb starkly cut through the fading light of the evening sky.

As Ramona guided the boat around to a cobbled together dock on the west side of the home, Eli noticed the home branched out into an aging double wide trailer on the north side. As the fishing boat's engine cut, he could hear the sound of another, similar motor nearby.

"Either they've been here, or the kid left the generator running this morning." Ramona scanned the length of her domain slowly.

Concerned the criminals might be around Eli moved to the ladder first. "Let us check things out first," he warned Ramona.

The old woman picked up her shotgun and racked it. "Don't you worry about me, son. This is my house."

"I'm sure you can handle yourself. But we're trained for this sort of thing," Dakota said.

"Listen missy. I've seen shit that would make you puke in your shoes," Ramona said. "So don't patronize me."

Dakota and Eli nodded almost in unison.

"I'm still gonna go first, if you'll let me." Eli had his hands on the rungs, but didn't want to climb until the old lady agreed. He was honestly afraid of what she might do.

Ramona nodded and Eli continued, pulling his gun as soon as he got up the ladder.

On top, he found a deck that matched the rest of the woman's home- mismatched colors and wooden scraps forming a frightening, yet somehow stable surface. One corner held a large grill made from a large barrel and supported by two or three rickety sawhorses. An old wiring spool took up one corner, surrounded by mesh chairs held together by duct tape. At the far end, a storm door led into the structure.

Once Ramona and Dakota made it to the deck, Eli asked, "Anything out of place here? Anything missing?"

"Door's open. But, shit, the kid can be a little careless." Ramona pointed to the metal door. Eli could see she was right; it hadn't been closed completely. It was a fact he'd missed in his quick scan.

Quietly opening the door, Eli stepped into the haphazard home. It was hard to tell if the place had been ransacked, or if it was exactly the way Ramona liked it. Yellowing newspapers were stacked waist high on either side of a narrow hall that led to the main living room, filling the air with their musty scent. As he advanced with his gun drawn, he encountered jars full of buttons and rocks on shelves, unidentified trinkets littering tables, and tins of fish hooks. The main room seemed to act as a hub to get a few steps down to the trailer section area straight ahead. At the bottom of the stairs an open door led to a cramped bathroom on the left.

"Up there, straight ahead in the kitchen," Ramona said.

The kitchen was equally as chaotic, with boxes of crackers and macaroni and cheese mixes on the counter, next to loaves of bread and sandwich buns. The sink was cluttered with silverware, fileting knives and cereal bowls.

When Eli turned to ask Ramona where they should look next, she said "This is it. Not much left other than some closets and a pantry."

"Where do you sleep?" Dakota asked. "We haven't seen a bed."

"Ah, there's a bed that folds down out of the closet over there. I sleep, I push the bed back up into the wall. Makes things a little more tidy that way." She pointed to what Eli assumed was a large pantry, with two dark wood doors set into the walls, before excusing herself to the bathroom for a few minutes.

"What next? Do we go back?" Dakota asked.

"No idea. This whole thing is so far out of bounds, my head is spinning," Eli said. They turned at the sound of flushing and water running from the bathroom.

"Well, no bank robbers in the can," Ramona joked. "Let's get moving."

"Okay," Dakota said. "Where else could the suspects have gone, if not here?"

It took Ramona a few minutes to answer as she roamed back to her kitchen. She grabbed a plastic grocery bag and tossed the box of crackers in, then a couple of bottles of water. "I'm guessing they didn't have many choices. Low fuel likely restricted their options. Unless they double-backed and got back on the road where you met me, there's only a few islands they could have landed on, and Ollie isn't stupid. He wouldn't keep going in the dark, he knows how bad things get out there."

"So, where does this information leave us?" Eli looked around the room again, wondering what else the old woman would throw into her bag.

A scraping across the shack's roof startled everyone.

"What was that?" Dakota asked.

The sound came again, a slow sweeping scratch, this time followed by multiple thuds.

"Is something up there? Or is it a loose shingle or something?" Eli looked for the obvious answers first.

From a drawer by the kitchen sink, Ramona pulled a revolver and quickly checked it. "I don't know what it is, and I don't have no loose tiles up there."

For a moment Eli pondered what he was more concerned about, the noise or Ramona. His curiosity got the better of him and he backtracked toward the door they came in, his own gun drawn. The floor creaked as he reached the stairs, and outright protested as he ascended toward the door.

The scraping noise stopped, but the thumping continued, indicating to Eli something was walking around up there. He pushed the door open slowly, doing his best to be silent. Outside, in the fading light, he made his way out onto the porch and looked around for signs of life there.

Behind him, he heard the thudding sound more clearly than inside. Eli turned as the scraping began again, and there, he was startled to see a pair of hunched over figures approaching him. His mind tried to make sense of the not-quite-human things there on the roof. They were short and covered with fur. Their round heads seemed too large to be held up by their thin necks. They stared at him with cold eyes as they came toward him on their hind legs, more human than animal. They crossed the roof in seconds, but hops and bounces. In the last few feet they gripped the drain spouting and lowered themselves on overly long arms and dropped to the deck with barely a sound.

Eli could only think to draw his gun and treat them like any other threat. "That's far enough. Stop right there." It was his training kicking in, and he could hear a voice in the back of his head telling him it was pointless to even try to talk to them.

"Who the hell are you talking to?" Ramona pushed open the door, startling the creatures.

Behind Ramona, Dakota pulled her sidearm as well. The shock on her face faded as one of the skunk apes sprung at her. The other creature jumped suddenly at Eli and he shot it twice, spinning the thin thing around as it fell. Nearly simultaneously, Dakota took similar action, knocking her attacker to the ground. This one didn't die as it landed on the wooden deck with a thud and screeched as it tried to get up and continue its assault.

"Don't waste your ammunition," Ramona said. She stepped forward and raised the butt of her shotgun before bringing it down on the thing's head with a crackle. "The smaller ones have thin skulls."

Ira and Dakota caught their breath from the sudden rush of the attack. But Ira was still aware enough of the situation to be impressed by Ramona's actions. After he caught his composure, he carefully bent down and looked closer at the skunk ape he'd killed. The overly-rounded head seemed to have too many teeth in it. He wasn't sure if it was his nerves or an actual fact the mouth seemed larger than it should have, leading to the abundance of yellowed teeth. He moved closer before the stench of the thing truly hit him.

Dakota moved around to the other side of the thing and pointed to an arm. "Just look how long the humerus bone is. That really makes its arms an extra four or five inches."

"And the fingers are more like a chimp or something. They're extended as well."

The two spent a few minutes examining the creature, poking it with a pen out of fear of touching the skunk ape directly.

"Let's move this along. I have a friend in trouble out there. You're not going to try to make me stay behind again, are you? Because it's not going to work out for you." Ramona stacked boxes of shotgun ammunition on the wobbly gas grill.

"Wouldn't think of it," Eli said. He figured if the older woman could survive out in the swamp with the gators and the snakes and these terrifying beasts, she could handle herself against a handful of bank robbers. He reloaded his gun and watched as Dakota checked her weapon as well.

"You don't have a phone out here? Something we can use to call for backup, let the locals know we need help?" Eli asked.

"Shit. What for? The government would use it to track me, plus they could send their mind control signals and make me do stuff." She scooped all of her ammunition into her bulging grocery bag. From what Eli could tell, there were steak knives, a meat cleaver, fileting knife and a Swiss army knife in there, and that was only what he could see.

"Okay, so maybe we take your boat back to find help? I mean, from the sounds of it, there's no way off the island, and they'll be stuck there." Dakota shrugged and looked at Eli. "What's the problem? Easy peasy."

"First of all, if we're going to work together, you need to never say 'Easy peasy' again," Eli said. "I really hate that phrase. And second, what's to keep them from leaving anyway, or what if they have someone coming to pick them up?"

Ramona laughed. "Plus, if you're going back to shore, you'll have to walk because I'm taking the boat to get Ollie back. *Good luck and fuck you very much.*"

She stepped around the dead skunk ape on the deck, grabbed her sack of frightening stuff and headed for the boat.

It was one of those moments Eli relished; he was getting his way thanks to someone else, rather than forcing his decision on the others. However, this little victory came with the footnote it was only achieved thanks to a lunatic lady with a shotgun. He pulled out his phone and waved it around looking for a signal, but failed to find one. He figured just because he got his way, it didn't mean he was stupid enough not to ask for help. If he could find a signal, he'd definitely call for backup.

"I checked everywhere as we were prepping. I couldn't get any bars either," Dakota said.

As they loaded back into the small boat, Eli stared at the hairy creatures on the deck. He'd heard about bigfoot and the Loch Ness Monster since he was a kid, but never really took much stock in the stories, he figured they were legends, exaggerations or flat-out lies. But the thing in the middle of the woman's rotting barbecue area was no hallucination. He thought again of all the other things it could be, but fell short. It wasn't an emaciated bear, not an oversized raccoon. He still wondered if it was a monkey, or something he wasn't familiar with, that escaped into the swamp and went rabid or something.

"You coming?" Dakota stood at the ladder to the boat. "Old Ramona's going to leave without us if she has her way."

"Sure."

"You still trying to figure this out?"

Eli nodded.

"Any luck?"

"Nope," Eli said, somewhat reluctantly. He stepped around the thing and crossed the patio right as Ramona started the motor of the little fishing boat.

10

"Let's go, you little shit." Stan yanked Ollie up by his arm and shoved him toward the side of the boat. "Get us up to this fucking mansion."

"Look, it's just up there beyond the trees. No one goes there anymore. It's falling apart. A death trap."

"Good, then nobody will bother us, will they?" Stan pushed him again.

"Leave me here. There's a path that leads right up to the house."

"You think we're leaving you with the boat, so you can take it the first chance you get?" Hank groaned as he stood up and got up in the kid's face. "You think we're stupid?" He waved his gun around wildly. "Do you?"

"Wait." As much as she wanted to take the boat and run herself, Lana took the opportunity to step in and maybe make a friend of the kid, in case she needed him to get out of the swamp. "Easy. Take it easy." She tugged back on Ollie to get him away from Hank. It wasn't hard. She could feel how easily he was led and guessed how weak he must be. "Just get us into the place. Get us in there safely and we can start to talk about how we're going to get you out of this and away from us, okay?" She smiled a little. She was exhausted from the insanity and tension of the job and the shit that followed. There was no way she felt like smiling, but she managed.

"I'm afraid…" Ollie said.

"We're all pretty worried about things right now. Trust me when I say we want it all over with. And it starts with you leading us down this path and getting us to the safest part of the house. We don't want to hurt you, so don't be afraid of us."

Ollie shrank back a little and spoke quietly. "It's not really you I'm worried about right now."

Lana thought about it for a moment, but before she could ask him why, Stan jumped in again.

"Let's go. Now." His voice was calm and somehow more frightening than when he was yelling.

Danny helped the kid up and handed him a flashlight from the boat.

They all helped Stan out of the boat and splashed through the water onto the muddy banks of the island. If there was a path here like the kid said, Lana didn't see it. There were only weeds, trees and muck. The place smelled like moss and still, fetid water.

Ollie reached down and picked up a thick branch, drawing an angry grunt from Hank.

"I need something to beat back these weeds. The path is pretty overgrown."

"You make sure you don't accidentally hit one of us," Hank said. He was leaning on Stan heavily and Lana hated seeing the two so close. It gave her a sense of unease that spread down her spine.

Ollie smacked away a clump of leaves hanging nearby and then another and another, using the limb as a machete. The others kept busy looking around themselves or back at the boat, but mostly they watched the kid carefully for signs of treachery.

Lana swatted at the insects buzzing around her head. They'd gotten worse once she stepped foot on the island. As she batted her hands around, she ran into a branch of wet leaves as they snapped back from one of the others letting it go ahead of her. "Shit." She kept reminding herself of the money. The money was all that mattered at this point. One of the backpacks was slung to her back and she could feel the heft of it, the reassuring weight of cold hard cash. Her foot sunk into mud and flooded her shoe with the sloppy sludge. With all the money, she could buy new shoes.

After a couple of minutes of slow pushing through the undergrowth, they came to a few steps that went up a bit, bringing them above most of the mud. The worst of it anyway. There was still no building in sight.

Soon, Ollie shouted he'd found the path. No one else would have dared call it an organized trail of any kind. It was more of an accidental line where there weren't any actual trees. Branches, leaves, bushes, everything else obscured the way, but Ollie managed to guide himself by it, much to the puzzlement of the others.

"Huh. This actually is a trail," Stan said. "I was pretty sure you were fucking with us, kid."

The trees and branches still grew thick on the path, hanging low enough that Danny and Hank had to duck a little bit just to be sure they weren't going to get stabbed in the eye by an errant twig or thorn.

The house was not exactly what Lana was hoping for… it had been described as an abandoned mansion, and it might have been true at one point. As they carefully balanced on the rotting dock, she could see one whole section of the building had collapsed long ago, and trees had grown through the floor there. Vines and other foliage took root as well, nearly obscuring the debris from the home completely.

"This? This is where you want to hide out?" Lana said. "Shit. I would rather have taken my chances making a run for it through Georgia or something. This thing looks like a location out of Scooby Doo or something."

"Fuck off." Hank stumbled onto the shore and swiped at the tall weeds with his rifle. "This is perfect. The highways are probably crawling with cops at this point."

Lana sighed. After they killed the man at the bank, the others at the convenience store and garage, the world was likely crawling with police, state troopers and every other member of law enforcement. "He's right, this place does scream 'cartoon villain' from the outside."

"Look, nobody saw us make our way out here. We're good."

Lana said, "What about the old lady?"

"Fuck the old Lady. What's she going to do?" Hank shouted. "She's not going anywhere and how is she going to find us anyway?"

Lana examined the rest of the house, and it didn't make her feel much better than the collapsed side. It was a large home, or it was at some point. The building was two stories, with a wide middle section and another wing like the collapsed one. None of the multitude of windows retained their glass. The paint peeled in wide curling sections that hung from the house like bark from an aging tree. The front doors hung from their hinges, crumbling onto the front porch.

Out of the corner of her eye, Lana noticed something as she was examining the house. The grass and other weeds leading to the front door appeared to be stomped down into a well-worn path. "Hey. It looks like someone has been here." She pointed out the trail to the others.

Stan bent down and looked at it more closely. "Probably an old path. Maybe some bums camped out in the house for a while. Or some hikers."

"They better be long gone by now, or they'll be sorry." Hank seemed weaker than before, and Lana hoped some sleep would help him. Otherwise, he was going to be a liability, slowing the group down when they finally decided to make their way back into civilization.

"The path looks newer to me." Ollie said.

"Just some animals, I'm sure." Stan pushed ahead toward the house.

Nearby, something snapped in the darkness.

"The fuck was that?" Stan stepped back, running into Lana.

"Get off me," Lana said.

"You heard the sound, right?" Stan waved his light around, blinding Lana in the process. She pushed him away and stepped to the side to avoid him.

Before anyone could admit whether they heard the same sound, a snarl erupted from the same area as the other sound, but this time, it became more than one sound, it was several creatures vocalizing at the same time.

There was no denying anything this time. The sound was real, and when Lana looked at the others, the fear and confusion was evident in their faces. They raised their guns, as several hairy beasts leapt from the bushes. There was little time to register what they were other than five foot tall, thin and scrawny. Their teeth registered with Lana, though. She definitely saw those. For such a small head, the things had large rounded teeth dripping with saliva as they snarled and lunged.

One of them bowled Stan over, sending both tumbling backward into the trees. He shouted and shot his pistol, sending the others to get out of his line of fire while also dodging the creatures as they came for them.

Lana and Danny shoved a creature away while looking for something to fight it with. Danny came up with a thick tree limb and swung it, bringing it down hard on their assailant's head.

"Hit it again," Lana shouted. She struggled to stay on her feet as the heavy backpack threatened to upset her balance and drop her on the ground.

Danny swung this time at the still-standing beast, connecting with its side and shattering the limb into a trio of splinters. The creature fell to the ground, a section of wood embedded in its side.

Hank shouted as he struggled with the other attacker. It was slashing at his face and chest, forcing the big man to retreat backward and protect himself with his arms, flailing wildly to get some advantage over the thing. His wound had opened up again, causing blood to spill out just as freely as after the gas station robbery.

Before Lana could try to use the heavy backpack as a weapon against the advancing creature, Danny got a running start and kicked the hairy beast. It didn't do a lot of damage, but it got the thing's attention and drew it away from their wounded uncle.

As both of them braced for it to zero in on them for new targets, the angry-looking beast was suddenly taken down by a trio of shots from Stan as he emerged from the nearby foliage. He was scraped across the chest and had a line of cuts down the right side of his face.

"Jesus." Stan put his hand to his face and dabbed at the blood there. "What the fuck is going on? What in the hell?" The blood streaked across his face as he patted it.

"Come on," Lana said. She could hear more growling in the weeds around them. "Where the fuck is that kid?" She grabbed Ollie by the t-shirt and pulled him closer. "Get us in the damn house. Now."

The kid didn't need to be asked twice. He was shivering and stumbled as he ran toward the mansion. Danny and Stan pulled Hank up and helped him move on, ignoring the blood covering him. The boy led them to a tattered porch, with boards missing and rotting rails. He grabbed the door handle and pushed, accidentally flinging it open easily and sending it slamming into the wall.

The others piled in behind him.

The room was filled with old, busted furniture, with a rotting couch placed nearly central in the space. Other splinters and shards of the building lay strewn around in piles, covered with dust and plaster from the drooping ceiling. A staircase on the opposite side led upstairs, but on closer inspection, there was only a framework left with zero steps and no railing.

Lana pushed in with the others and closed the door as best she could. One of the hinges was nearly falling off and the other looked like it was on its last legs.

"What the fuck were those things, man?" Stan knelt next to one of the cracked windows and looked out into the night.

"How the hell should we know?" Hank sat himself gently down on the disgusting couch and grabbed his side. "Shit. That fucking hurts."

Lana sat on the floor, pushing some debris away to make a relatively clean spot. Her heart beat so hard she swore it was shaking her whole body back and forth as it did. She felt nauseous and more than a little dizzy as she thought of the things outside. Her brother paced back and forth, stopping only to glance out the nearest window, his pistol in hand.

Her immediate thought was escape. Escape from the house, escape from the things in the swamp, escape from the police; whatever got her out of her current situation and somewhere safe. To that end, she swept the house without moving from the floor. The house was as bad and terrifying on the inside as it was from the outside. The windows not boarded up showed jagged bits of glass or shredded curtains covering them. The floors, filthy with decades of mud and dirt, were rotting and soft in places. The stairs leading to the second floor were surely deathtraps, missing boards and railing. One of the halls led off into darkness and the two doors in the room appeared to be holding on to their hinges by splinters and rusted metal.

The stench of the place was what hit Lana the hardest. She placed the underlying smells of rotting wood and vegetation easily. They were simple to guess, taking in the look of everything around her. There was something else permeating the room. She'd first caught it right before they took the boat, and it reappeared stronger once they approached the house. Inside, it was thick.

"You smell it too?" Her brother approached her. "The fuck is that? Did something shit in here?"

"Why the fuck do you think they call them skunk apes?" Stan said. "It ain't for their hygiene and bathing habits. They stink."

Ollie stood up, happy for the distraction of conversation. "But, it's so strong in here, and none of them are close."

"Maybe it's their den. Maybe they live here and we're intruding on their territory." Stan held his knife close to his side and looked at the others. "If this is their home, they sure as hell aren't going away any time soon."

"Their home? That's crazy. They're swamp creatures, they don't live in goddamn mansions." Hank groaned and grabbed his side. Lana got up from the floor and walked over to him, gently lifting his arm away so she could see the wound.

"This is bad. It's bad and sure as hell not getting any better."

"It'll be fine." Hank said.

Lana grimaced and pulled the old bandage off. It wasn't fine, she was sure of that. She pulled a new wad of gauze from the boat's kit and applied it quickly. "Hold this," she said to Danny. She packed as much as she could over the wound before taping it down. There was a lot of blood seeping through the thin gauze almost immediately. "You need a doctor."

"No shit."

"So, what's going on?" Stan asked. "What are we going to do here?"

"We stick with the original plan," Hank said. "We wait here for Lucas. He'll be here tomorrow afternoon to pick us up and we get the fuck out of here. Start livin it up on the French Riviera or some shit."

"Sounds like an incredibly vague plan." Danny was sweating despite the cool evening air. "How are we getting out of the country so easily?"

"Don't worry about it. Lucas is a friend. He'll do us right." Stan went back to the window and peered out.

"How is Lucas going to do that? Aren't we in the wrong place?" Lana smelled bullshit in their well-thought-out plan. Nothing was going right, so why should it start suddenly thanks to Lucas?

"Don't worry. He's not an idiot." Stan said.

The conversation stopped, leaving Lana to wipe her bloody hands on her jeans and stand up. She crossed the room to her brother, slightly concerned by each creak and groan of the floorboards. "Let's take a walk around the place," she told him. She grabbed at his elbow and all but led him away.

"Don't go far," Stan said.

"We don't plan to."

They stepped carefully over blackened boards and broken furniture. They nearly stumbled on great chunks of plaster and paint from the ceiling as they crossed to the open wall leading them to the dining area, then the open kitchen. It was just as terrible as the other rooms, with broken cabinet doors and rusted skillets, shards of broken dishes littered every surface. Here, there was fading graffiti, likely from the few that had dared to wander into the swamp in search of something to deface.

"So, what the hell?" She kept her voice down for fear it would carry throughout the house. "We can't stay here, right? Those things nearly killed us on the way in, what if they bust through the door, or the windows or something? This fucking house is about as stable as cardboard."

"And what about Hank? He can't move fast if we need to leave. We should stay and wait for Lucas. We can hold out here for a day, I think."

Lana shook her head. "I'm just worried about holding out for the night. We've only got a few lights from the boat, and our cell phones. This place is a death trap in the dark. Plus, we're going to be lucky if Hank lives to get picked up. He's still losing blood and the first aid kit isn't doing shit for him."

"And?"

"And... and we need to leave. Fight our way back to the boat and get back to dry land asap. We still have a little daylight out there, at least we can get away from this house and out into the swamp before we lose it." Lana looked at the disaster around them. "We never should have come here; we never should have listened to Hank just because he's family."

"Easy to say now. The money sounded good when we were planning this thing."

He wasn't wrong, but Lana didn't want to admit it. The money they grabbed was great, but if they didn't live to spend it, what was the point? "Let's have a look around and see if there's a safer room or something to help us barricade the doors and windows."

They continued through the kitchen, crunching on broken glass and dishes as they went. Beyond that, the house somehow managed to get worse. There, in a long hallway, the wall was demolished in such a fashion the outside was creeping in. A massive hole in the center of the wall was only partially visible through the trees and bushes that made their way inside. Even in the dim light, Lana could see the muddy tracks littered across the floor, some heading away down the hall, the rest covering the floor heading toward them.

Lana flipped her phone's light on and shined it onto the rotting wood below their feet. "Shit. Look at all these footprints."

"They ain't human," Danny said. "Look at the way the toes are spread out." He touched the dirt around the prints and brought his hand back, rubbing the grit between his fingers. "Most of these are pretty old, they're dry."

Lana moved her light further down the hall. "Yeah, but those aren't." Ahead, the hall was covered in mud, fresh leaves and pools of water.

"Did they come in when we did?"

Lana shook her head. "No clue."

"Are they still here?"

That was the question stuck in Lana's mind as they moved down the hall into the unknown.

The hall ended at a staircase leading down to the lower level. There may have been a door there at one time, but it was long gone, the entire wall smashed away with it. Lana paused and waved her phone back and forth, trying to get the dim light on it to show her more. All she could make out was the presence of worn stairs and a cracked railing, both of which disappeared into the void below.

"I'm not going down there," Danny said. "Fuck that. Not if all four of us went in together. Not if the damn marines were with us."

A cold draft blew up to greet the pair, a welcome sensation after the stifling Florida sun, though the smell it brought with it was less than comforting. It smelled like those terrible creatures outside. Rotten eggs, body odor, shit. It wasn't a pleasant aroma, and it made Lana's knees buckle just a bit. She agreed with her brother completely. There was no way she was going down there without a flamethrower or a rocket launcher. Still, she wanted to know how much to worry about what waited for them down below.

Part of her answer came quickly. As she was about to suggest they rejoin the others and tell them what they'd found, she heard a sound in the basement and held her hand up to Danny to have him be quiet. He looked cross, but did as she asked, folding his arms as he waited.

In the space below them, she heard the distinct sound of water. It wasn't dripping or pouring, it was more like sloshing. Something was moving through the swamp water collected in the building's lowest level.

"Did you hear that?" Lana asked as the noise stopped.

"Maybe it's a leak from the rain collected somewhere after the storm?"

Her head was shaking before she'd really thought about it. "No. It stops and starts. It sounds like it's moving through the room down there."

"Nah," Danny said. "You think those things are down there? They can't be. There would be a lot more noise, right? They'd all be making splashing sounds." He didn't look convinced to Lana.

"Let's just go. Regroup with the others and figure this out." She backed up, her light still shining on the dark passageway leading down. "But if the cops show up to arrest us? I'm not hiding down there. No way."

"Same."

The brother and sister cautiously made their way back, avoiding the hole in the wall, stepping lightly. Lana couldn't help but think this was the worst place they could have gone into hiding ever. They would have been better off stealing a new car and driving east until they got to the ocean, then swam for it. Instead, they worked their way into an impossible situation and started sinking deeper with each passing hour.

Back in the main room, Stan was still pacing and peering out each window he passed. "Where did you two go?"

"Looking for a way out, or a good place to hole up." Lana said.

"And?"

Lana looked behind her at the hallway and stifled a shiver. "No. In fact, we're worried those things are in the basement."

"What?" The announcement got Stan to stop pacing. "What are you talking about? Where?"

Pointing a finger at the floor, Danny said, "Basement. Right below us."

Hank couldn't even speak. He stammered and blustered until he finally gave up.

"You saw them?" Ollie sat up straighter on the couch.

"No. But we found tracks and we heard something moving downstairs in the water."

"Shit. There could be an alligator down there that got trapped or something." Hank shook his head and leaned back on the filthy piece of furniture. "You two are just jumpy."

"*Just jumpy*? Holy shit, we were almost killed by a bunch of filthy stinking monsters. How are you NOT jumpy? How are you not running through the swamp barking like a dog at what we saw out there?"

11

"Maybe you two can make yourselves useful and find a way to board up some of those windows so we don't have anything crawling through them in the middle of the night," Stan said. He clutched his gun to his chest tightly.

"Can't you help with that?" Lana asked.

"I'm standing watch." He nodded over to Hank, who'd fallen asleep on the nasty couch. "He sure ain't going to be any help at all."

Lana nudged Danny. "Maybe we can scrounge up some wood to cover the worst ones?"

"We don't have a hammer or anything. How are we going to secure whatever we find?"

Lana leaned close to her brother. "Who the fuck cares, let's get them covered."

"I can help," Ollie said. I can at least find some boards. I'm certainly not going to run for it. Not in the dark and not after seeing those things." He tagged along behind the siblings without a comment from anyone.

The three came to a disused stairway leading up at the first hall. The steps were half missing or busted. Lana was sure there was no way to get up to the second floor without a lot of luck or some sort of terrible death wish.

"Think we can rip some of these stairs out and use them to block some of the windows?" Danny asked.

"Why not? It should give us a decent supply." Lana pointed to a few of the loose pieces of the banister. "Ollie, can you tear those off?" The kid seemed somewhat grateful to have something to do. Lana figured he was probably happy to not be near Stan or Hank. At least she and her brother treated him with some sort of concern. The other two were fully prepared to kill him if his usefulness ran out, and they did nothing to hide the fact.

The kid yanked until the wood came apart.

"Here," Danny said. "You two rip some of this up and I'll make a pile in the other room." He disappeared with an armload of scrap wood.

Once Danny was out of sight, Lana asked, "You okay?"

"What?"

"I'm only seeing how you're handling things, that's all."

The kid kicked one of the splintered steps a couple times before answering. "It's not great. I'm a little freaked out."

"Yeah. Makes sense. Listen, I..." Lana was cut short by a sudden rumble as part of the stairs gave way and fell into the floor with a crunch of rotted wood. She steadied herself as the floor under her feet began to buckle with the sudden weight of the debris. "Holy shit, Ollie run."

They both took a couple of steps to run away, but a huge section of the floor dropped away, taking them along with it. Lana had the wind knocked out of her as she landed hard on the crumbled wood.

Lana sat up quickly and strained to see what was around her. The light from the hole in the ceiling cast a pale glow from what she guessed was thirty feet up.

"Hey," Danny shouted. "Are you okay down there?"

She moaned in reply, discovering as she moved, she'd done some damage to her shoulder in the fall. "Mostly."

"What about the kid?"

"Don't know." Lana felt around, waiting for her eyes to adjust. "Hey? Are you okay?" Slowly the room came into focus, exposing bare rock walls and a muddy, wet floor. They'd fallen into a space much smaller than the main room they'd come from. Lana figured it was maybe ten feet by ten feet, if the shadows weren't playing tricks on her. Behind her, she saw a dilapidated wooden door. Small pinholes of light pushed through cracks and holes in the slats.

"Uhhhn."

"Kid?" Lana asked. She crawled through the muck in the direction of the sound. Soon, a mud-caked arm rose from the darkness. "Ollie? Are you hurt?"

"I don't know." He spit to the side several times. "Where are we?"

"Don't know, can't see enough to figure out what this room was, but it's pretty trashed at this point." Lana found the boy and touched his arm to let him know she was there. "Take it slow when you sit up, we fell pretty hard." While the room was getting clearer with her vision adjusting, Lana couldn't see what they were stuck in the room with. In addition to the skunk apes, she supposed the swamp had all manner of snakes, gators and other messed up creatures which would love a dark, damp place like this.

"How the hell are we going to get you out of there?" Danny looked down at the pair, brow furrowed and eyes narrowed. "Is there a ladder down there or something?"

"A twenty-foot ladder? Down here?" Lana sighed. "No. Is there rope up there?"

"Maybe in the boat."

"Ugh."

Danny gingerly peered over the edge. "Shit, we found the set of stairs earlier, right? Just come up over there."

"We also heard something moving at the bottom of the steps, you know? Something we may want to avoid." Lana wanted to throw something at the guy. "Other options?"

The kid patted her on the arm. "If you heard something down here, maybe we shouldn't be yelling? I mean, I'm sure our crash through the floor created enough of a ruckus, but maybe we shouldn't continue fucking shouting back and forth like this?"

"Yeah. That's… that's probably true." She tried to force the initial panic and pain of the situation to drain from her body, to calm herself, but only partially succeeded as she felt the shaking in her hands only slow down instead of stop.

"Okay?" Ollie asked

Lana nodded, breathing deeply, and exhaling loudly. "Let's see if we can get to the door and figure out what's on the other side. Then we can decide what to do next." She felt for her phone, hoping to get a little more light for the precarious journey of just a few feet. When she didn't find it in her front pocket, she tried her back pants pocket and all of the ones in her jacket.

"Shit." She felt around in the mud and dirt where she'd fallen with zero luck.

"What?" Ollie asked.

"No phone."

"So?"

"No phone, no light." Her hands were covered in mud, which she tried to wipe off on her jacket as best she could. "Light would be nice right about now."

While Lana cleaned herself up, Ollie moved away, becoming a shadow in the dim glow through the door and the hole overhead. She heard him slop through mud and bump into objects along the way, but soon he blotted out what little light made it through the holes in the door.

Lana got up and resigned herself to moving on without the phone. She figured it would be in their best interest if they got out sooner, rather than later. If any of those things heard the noise, they'd come looking for the source. Considering they were unarmed and injured, Lana didn't want to be there when they got there.

She looked up at the men looking on from the floor above and said, "We're going to check things out. Maybe we can get up the steps without getting too close to anything." She whispered as loud as she could and hoped her brother got the jist of things.

At the door, she put her hand on Ollie's shoulder just to get an idea of where he was, and put her eye up to one of the numerous holes. The area beyond was illuminated by light that streamed in from a huge hole caused by what looked like the collapse of the rock and mud wall on the far side. Water pooled at the center of the larger room, trees took root in the floor and reached up with sun hungry branches. The light was a bright orange and Lana guessed darkness was only a few minutes off. The floor was littered with leaves, weeds and junk. More trash left from the house's heyday and the tenure of whatever vandals had tagged the rooms upstairs.

"It looks empty," Lana said.

The kid agreed, "Yeah, but there's an open doorway on the other side. Kind of wish I knew if there was anything down there."

Lana hadn't noticed the hall. It was dark and partially covered by vines, weeds and debris. "Maybe we could climb out of the hole in the wall?"

"It's possible, but I don't know if we should. That's a mud wall on the other side of the stones. Probably goes all the way up to the first floor? It's what, twenty-five, thirty feet up?" He took a deep breath and sighed. "I don't like the odds of either of us making it without a rope or a ladder."

It was tough for Lana to disagree with him. She had trouble standing up at their current location, she couldn't imagine the odds of them both being able to climb a mud wall thirty feet into the marshlands. That left exploring the lower level for a way out as their only other hope.

"Well, let's see if we can get out there without drawing more attention to ourselves. We're not going to find a way out by standing around." Lana felt around the door for a handle, turning it once she did. Unfortunately, the door didn't budge when she pushed on it gently. She switched gears and pulled, worried the floor would block it either way.

"Stuck? I mean it's been here long enough, maybe some of the mud rose high enough to block it?"

Ollie leaned hard against the door and Lana felt it give a little. "I think you've got it. Let's try again," she said. Their combined efforts made the door move slowly through the slop of the floor on the other side. She pushed her arm through and used her leverage to push it more until she could get through. The kid was slightly smaller than she was, so it only made sense that he would fit if she did.

They both stood in the mucky wet room, which looked pretty much as they'd seen it through the holes, except they couldn't see the extent of the junk along the walls. It was stacked halfway up the wall on one side: old rusty bedsprings, shattered dresser, glass lantern shards, torn clothing and tree limbs. It forced the pair to stand closer to the pit of water in the middle of the area. While she was pretty sure it wasn't very deep, the murky pit made Lana uneasy, like the hole went down to the center of the earth and creatures of all manner could crawl out and menace the world at any minute, starting with her and the kid.

12

"Look. It's getting dark out here, maybe we should slow down a touch," Eli shouted over the roar of the outboard motor. "I mean, I'd rather not crash this thing and have to wade through the swamp the rest of the way."

"I know this marsh like the back of my hand." Ramona held her place at the back of the boat like a stone statue, never flinching at the occasional spray from the bow, not even stealing a glance to see if the mass they'd nearly hit was a rock or a gator. Eli was inclined to trust her no matter what his personal fears might be.

"How far?" Dakota yelled.

Ramona shrugged. "I don't know. Fifteen minutes, maybe. Haven't been out there in some time. Didn't seem like a smart thing to do."

Eli felt his stomach drop like a rock, partially at Ramona's boating skills and partially at the implications of her words. "You think there's more of those things?"

"Been telling the law about it for years."

When Eli glanced at Dakota, she shrugged. "Sorry. It sounded crazy. So, we never got around to chasing that report down. I told you they sent me on some calls as a joke."

The boat veered into taller weeds and Eli ducked to keep from getting slapped in the face by the leaves. As he recovered, the boat's motor sputtered to silence.

"What's up? I thought we were ten minutes or more away?" Dakota asked.

It was hard to misread the concerned look on Ramona's face. "Up there." She pointed to a stretch of land parallel to the boat's course. There, half out of the water was the largest gator Eli had seen in the Glades. He guessed it to be nearly fifteen feet long and several feet wide. Before he could ask what they should to avoid the thing, he noticed there was something wrong with it.

As they drifted past, he saw the other side of the huge beast was mangled and bloody. Its front leg was gone and the skin was torn off down to the bone around its head.

"The hell?" Dakota asked. "What happened here?"

"I'm betting it was them," Ramona said.

"Them? Them who?" Eli looked at the old woman and then went back to marveling at the gator. "Them? The skunk apes? Are you shitting me? How is that possible? With that huge thing, there would have to be dozens of skunk apes. More." He turned to Ramona and discovered her face hadn't changed expression.

Dakota noticed too, "How many of these things are out there, Ramona?"

"No idea."

"But it's a lot, isn't it?" Eli asked.

Ramona nodded and started the motor up again. "We need to hurry up if we're going to catch up with these bastards."

For a moment, Eli wondered whether she meant the criminals or the apes, but decided it didn't really matter.

"We stay away from the old mansion because they took it over. It's theirs now. Has been for some time. Anyone dumb enough to venture in there finds out real quick whose kingdom it is."

The boat jerked forward causing Eli and Dakota to brace themselves to keep from falling over.

"If they claim the place, what are they doing this far away?" Dakota asked.

"Rain's been sparse last couple of years. Their hunting ground is dying off, the grasses, the animals, all of it. They need to get out further to find food." Ramona spoke loud enough to be heard over the boat and the waves. "That's why I called you out recently. They were stealing my catches from the traps. If they got used to it, they'd get territorial out this way too. Can't have that." She adjusted the boat's spotlight and pushed the motor harder.

As the darkness dropped on the small boat, Eli decided not to ask more questions. He really didn't want to know more about the beasts. It started off weird and got progressively more terrifying. There was no way he could have guessed when he got up that morning, he'd chase a lead on his spate of bank robberies which would pull him to a kidnapping and skunk apes. Although, he thought, who really does expect their day to take that kind of turn?

He and Dakota both took out their cell phones and did their dance of waving them around in the air, looking for a signal. He didn't know about Dakota, but he would love to be able to call someone for backup, preferably many someones with many guns. But after they both scanned for a signal, they came up empty.

After a few minutes, Ramona pointed excitedly ahead. "There."

Dakota and Eli looked at the thick patch of reeds ahead of them which looked like all the other reeds they'd crashed through in the past half hour.

"What?" Eli asked.

"Look," Ramona pointed again. "See how those are darker? They're wet. Someone ran them down when they were cruising through here. And not all that long ago. We're going in the right direction." She swung the boat around and crashed headlong into the tall grass, scanning for similar guidelines.

"Seriously?" Eli asked. The brush all looked the same to him, he couldn't find any extra-wet or darker strands, it all blended in. But Ramona appeared to be on to something and that was all that mattered. Without her, Eli admitted to himself, they would still be on shore, maybe even at the police barracks with their hands in their pockets and zero leads. Of course, this jaunt through the swamp could be a waste of time, but at least they were keeping themselves busy.

After another ten minutes of tight turns and sudden stops, Ramona cut the dinghy's engine and they drifted slowly toward the island. The hulk of the old mansion could be seen in between the enormous trees dotting the shore.

"No lights?" Dakota asked.

"I don't see anything, but I guess there's no surprise there. They'd want to lay low, keep as hidden as possible." Eli focused on the windows of both the main and second floors, hoping to catch the pale beam of a cell phone, or a candle's flicker, but found nothing.

Once they got close enough to land, Eli hopped out and splashed through the water, pulling the boat ashore.

"You might want to be careful doing that," Ramona said. "Coulda been gators waiting in the water for you. Gobble you up if you're not careful."

"Really?" Eli looked around him on the shore and in the water, looking for beady eyes and flipping tails.

"Kind of late now, wouldn't you say?" Ramona stepped self-assuredly onto the beach, shotgun in hand.

Dakota motioned to the others and pointed her flashlight at a larger craft a hundred yards up the beach.

"My boat," Ramona said. "What did those monsters do to her?"

As they approached, it was evident it had been trashed, with the canopy itself hanging torn and tattered off the frame, bits of the vehicle were torn off and tossed in the swamp around it. Eli couldn't tell if the damage included an attack on the people who had been passengers on the boat, or whether it happened after they'd disembarked.

"Those sons of bitches," Ramona said. "Look what they did to my *Marsh Mellow*. They've torn it apart. They've fucked it up bad."

It was Florida, after all. Maybe her insurance covered skunk ape attacks. Eli was sure he didn't want to ask.

The trio gathered around the *Marsh Mellow* and examined it. A foot of water collected in the stern. It had most certainly been torn up, but likely not by the bank robbers. The seats had what appeared to be claw marks through them, same with the hull. Various instruments were torn from their dash, cracked and broken on the ground. A long crack along the starboard side made it clear the things wouldn't make it out on the water again anytime soon.

"Oh god." Ramona's eyes narrowed. "These things don't do shit like this. Not unless they're provoked. These criminals of yours must be real assholes."

It made Eli wonder how Ramona thought she knew the wild beasts so well she could predict their behavior in any given situation. He'd figured her for the kooky swamp lady early on, but he'd revised his assessment slightly seeing how she'd managed to live on her wits out in the unforgiving marshes for so long.

"Well, if these idiots we're chasing somehow disturbed their home while looking for a hideout, that might be a good reason, don't you think?" Dakota picked up a flare gun kit from the boat and checked it before sliding it into her pack. "Alright. There's somewhat of a trail here. Do we want to make our way to the house?"

Before Eli could agree, Ramona held one hand up to stop them, then shushed them. From the west side of the house the gentle sound of leaves in the breeze grew like a cyclone. The noise became mixed with growls and snorts and the grass made way for a trio of skunk apes as they charged out of the foliage twenty yards ahead of Eli.

Ramona's shotgun was up and she fired before Eli and Dakota managed to clear their weapons from their holsters. The lead skunk ape fell, sliding across the mud and weeds. The other two charged, leaping over their fallen companion without a glance. Eli fired two shots, clipping one on the shoulder and putting another bullet through its forearm. The beast howled and fell to the ground, still alive. The third dropped to the ground, thanks to Dakota's marksmanship.

"Fuck," Eli looked at the writhing creature before him. "Should we save it? I mean, no one is going to believe this. Should we keep it for proof?" He stared at it, feeling revulsion wash over him as he tried to make sense of the creature before him. He thought he understood why they called it an ape, as it definitely had qualities of a primate. But he also saw some somewhat human properties in the thing as well, and that was where he had trouble reconciling what he was seeing. Was it possible the thing was a stunted human of some kind? Could it be a feral child or something?

A shotgun blast tore the last one apart, sending blood and guts flying. "There are plenty more coming if you feel like starting a collection." Ramona ejected the shells from her double barrel and put in two more. "Believe me, you don't want to have a pissed off, injured skunk ape behind you when you don't have to."

"You seem to know a lot about this, considering these things shouldn't exist," Dakota said.

"And you two don't seem to know shit about shit. So, maybe pay attention and you'll learn as you go." Ramona stepped onto the faint path and waved the two others on. "I find it hard to believe these critters would only send three little shits after us."

"How many do you think there are?" Eli asked. His mind reeled at the thought there could be many more.

"No idea. I've never been *in* their nest before."

Eli stopped Ramona with a hand on her elbow. "Nest?"

"Did I stutter?" She moved on, shrugging his hand off of her.

"How do you know all this?" Dakota asked.

"I know a lot of things. Learned them working for the government for a while before I retired." She moved without using a flashlight or any other means to illuminate her path.

"The government?" Eli was taken aback by the suggestion the strange swamp woman ever worked for Uncle Sam. "What branch?"

"Damn, you never stop yapping, do you?"

Eli could hear Dakota snicker a little at the other woman's cranky reply. He turned off his flashlight and slid it in his back pocket, hoping the move would help them not be so easily spotted if the suspects were waiting anywhere nearby. He was sure their own gunfire had alerted the bank robbers already.

For a flash, Eli wondered again who it was Ramona had worked for in the Federal government. Imaging her as a NAVY SEAL was a nice distraction from the position Eli found himself in.

13

Lana and Ollie crept closer to the dark hallway, stepping around the trash scattered around. When they could see, they realized the hall led down to more rooms and more darkness. There, at the mouth of the hall, Lana encountered the smell again. The terrible stench that wafted up the stairs when they explored the first floor and paused at the stairs. It was equally horrible at the hallway, hitting them both hard enough to make them step back, and causing the kid to gag.

"I thought you'd seen these things before?" Lana asked.

"Doesn't make them any more pleasant-smelling." He took a few deep breaths and covered his nose with the crook of his elbow. "Fuck. Excuse my language."

"You're good. If ever there was a situation or smell which called for cursing, this is the place and time."

They pushed forward, down the long hall until they came to a door on their right. It was nearly as rotted and terrible as the last, and felt wet to Lana's touch, much like everything else down there. She pointed to it to let Ollie know she was going to try to open it and he nodded acknowledgement. The knob felt loose the moment she touched it, but before she could let go the heavy metal orb fell off in her hand, with a half dozen other parts splashing to the wet ground. She and Ollie cringed and waited to hear if the noise brought any of the creatures or anything else moving in their direction.

After a moment, the both breathed easy and Ollie bent down to look through the hole in the door where the handle had been. "Nothing in there. Looks a lot like the room we left," he whispered. "Bunch of junk. Busted stuff."

The next doorway was missing its door completely, which made Lana happy. They didn't have to go through the ordeal of opening a door again.

Inside was much like the others with garbage and rotting furniture, except this time they found a rusting bed frame with exposed springs from the mattress.

Ollie reached into the pile of cast-off material and pulled out a twisted cross bar that had been snapped at about two feet. "This might make a good weapon. Better than nothing at least." Lana thought about whether she wanted their potential hostage carrying a sharp metal stick around, but decided the risk of him killing her down there was minimal. He was still on edge and she hoped, smart enough to realize they would need to help each other if they wanted out of this.

"Yeah. Good idea. See if there's another one for me," Lana pushed some things around until they found another, somewhat smaller, chunk of metal. It reminded her of a prison shiv, sharp and easily concealed. "Okay." I truly don't feel much safer, but it's the best we have, I suppose."

Ollie tore one of the sleeves off of his sweatshirt and wrapped it around one end, creating a handle for holding the jagged weapon a little easier. "Here," he tore a long strip off and tossed it to Lana. "Maybe we won't get tetanus or whatever."

"Not the highest thing on my list of shit I was worried about, but sure." She looked at the kid as she wrapped cloth around her makeshift knife. It was hard for her to tell if he was smart or just used to a tough life working out in the marsh, where shit could kill you on an hourly basis. Maybe tetanus was something he had to worry about on the regular. Lana wasn't even positive if she's ever had a tetanus shot ever in her life.

As they finished wrapping their weapons, they heard a sudden splash, followed by more in the hall. Ollie's eyes went wide and Lana motioned for him to get against the wall next to the doorway immediately. She did the same on the other side. Peering out from the dark room she could see one of the skunk apes rushing toward them. It moved quickly through the muddy passage without slipping or slowing. Lana watched the beast's lanky frame glide forward effortlessly. The long thin hair was caked in muck and leaves from rounded head to bare feet. While the arms were thin, they still showed muscular definition, giving her even more reason to fear the beast. As it passed, it stopped at the hole in the wall further back and climbed easily out, stretching its arms out and pulling itself along. It disappeared in seconds.

Before they could even exhale at the close call, more of the monsters came charging from the same direction. Three of them this time, with the same frame, same general build, but one of them seemed a lighter shade of brown than the others, or maybe it was only slightly less caked in water, dirt and leaves. The trio appeared and left as quickly as the first one had.

"Sweet Jesus, those things are nasty," Lana said. "How many of them do you think there really are?"

"I couldn't tell you. But I'm afraid the longer we stay here, the more likely we are to find out."

They both took deep breaths and Lana said, "Ready?" When Ollie nodded, she stepped out first, looking both ways down the hall before continuing down the hall. It was just as sloppy and gross as the rest of the way had been, and the next door they came to was blocked by debris and weeds. It saved them the trouble of trying to open it and draw attention to themselves, but it gave them one less place to hide if they needed it.

The pair stayed to the sides of the larger room, carefully staying out of the water, making as little noise as possible. Ahead of them, the next room teemed with commotion. Somewhere around there was the stairwell that led back up. Lana was confused enough she wasn't sure if the stairs were after the next room, in it, or right before it.

Ollie whispered, "How many do you think are in there? They're making a fuck ton of noise."

"No clue. Let's just get around them and be done with it." Lana leaned against the wall. "Unless you have a better idea?"

Lana wished they could be done with it already. They hadn't tried any other means of escape, maybe they try something else first? The ceilings were too high for them to climb up to unless they stacked some of the junk scattered around. That would make far too much noise and attract attention. The skunk apes climbed through a hole in the wall earlier. That was a possible point of exit, but they already knew there were creatures, and whatever else outside to contend with.

"I can't think of another easy way out," Ollie said.

"There isn't one." It still irked Lana the others had suddenly moved away from the hole that opened up and dropped the pair through. They could have dropped a line or something down to pull her up or something. Still, they ran away from the opening without a word leaving her and Ollie to fend for themselves in the dark.

She motioned to Ollie to follow her through the doorway quietly, and he nodded his approval. They stepped carefully over the stone floor and moved ahead into the new room. The sound of the creatures got louder here, the chaos of the skunk apes growling and stamping nearly in unison becoming like a wave through the subfloor. There was a glimmer of light that fed through from above and Lana caught the shadows of half a dozen of the creatures moving and loping around the other side of the building, thankfully unaware of the pair of intruders making their way along the walls.

The creatures walked more like humans than any kind of ape Lana had seen, though there was something about their gait set them apart, maybe the way their thin legs carried them so lightly. She found their pacing strange for a wild creature. She stopped and watched for a moment, trying to gauge their process or their meaning. It looked for all she could guess, that they were waiting for something.

Just beyond the pacing skunk apes, there was a room with a large dark shape inside. It looked like more debris piled high, but it was impossible to tell. The faint light only gave Lana a shape and size, but no details.

The door they were looking for was close.

Ollie started walking again, slowly, their escape only a few feet ahead. As long as the creatures continued their distracted movements, it wouldn't be a problem. Eyes locked on their only potential stumbling blocks, Lana stepped into the alcove at the bottom of the stairs and pulled Ollie with her. They stood for a moment, letting their eyes adjust to the light, only to find there was a much worse problem.

The stairs were mostly gone from about the midpoint down to the floor. There were still a few of those intact, but they looked to be hanging on by splinters. The top few looked whole, but Lana couldn't assess their condition from so far down and in the dark. There was still somewhat of a banister on both sides, but it was in sorry shape as well.

"Look." Lana thought about their situation and, against her better judgment, said, "Okay. You go first, if you think you can do it. I'll stay here and see what I can do to distract them, or help you or whatever." She still had the thorn in her side about Stan and Hank forcing the kid to come with them.

Normally she'd be all about being first and saving herself, but the stupid kid had made her care about him or something.

"I don't know if I can do this." Ollie looked up to the top.

"Not much choice."

"I suppose."

"I mean, look, if you want me to go first, I'm fine with it," Lana said. They probably weighed the same, she thought. He was shorter than her, but had a little more heft.

With a deep breath, Ollie said, "I'll give it a try." Maybe I can find the safest way for you as I go."

Lana turned back to look at the creatures and immediately heard the rotten wood creak under the weight of the kid's first step. It was followed by an immediate staccato of quiet cursing from the kid. The creatures were making so much noise they didn't seem to hear the sound or the language, and went about their business without missing a step.

She looked behind her to check out Ollie's progress, finding he'd only gone up the equivalent of three stairs. He walked on the base of the railing sometimes, as it seemed to be fairly secure. He tiptoed and tested his moves, pushing on the boards with his toes and shaking the banister to make sure it was secure with each step.

"You're doing great." The encouragement came from her mouth like someone else had said it. She turned back to monitor the skunk apes only to find they'd stopped moving and stared into the dark room beyond them. And to Lana's surprise, the big mound she assumed was garbage moved. With what looked like two simple movements, it pulled itself through the doorway and stepped into the dim light.

Lana gasped at the sight of the new creature revealed in the dim light. It was much like the skunk apes, but larger. The long hair covering its body seemed to be a silvery gray, making it appear older and more haggard than the rest. Her best guess was it stood seven foot tall, nearly two feet taller than most of the others. It moved slowly as the others walked around it. Where the skunk apes had terrified her from the beginning, this one was enough to make her knees go weak, and she ducked back into the stairwell to keep from being seen.

"*Oh, shit,*" she whispered. "*You need to climb faster.*"

14

The sounds of the skunk apes filled the night sky, seeming to come from everywhere.

"I think our shooting must have stirred them up, people. Stay on your toes, they'll all come running when they think they have a chance," Ramona said.

Again, Eli wondered what made her an expert on the beasts. "Any idea what the best way in would be? I mean, can we avoid these things?"

"Well, I ain't been here since forever. And I have no idea where these cryptid bastards are coming from. I got nothing," Ramona said. "I think we go for the front door and hope for the best."

"That's not a real plan, you know." Dakota said. She covered the rear of the group, and Eli was happy to let her. If she had half the skills he thought she did, there was nothing to worry about from behind them. It was the uncertainty ahead of them that worried him.

Eli shrugged. They were both right. They had no plan, so going in the front door was the best way to go. If they took the time to circle the building looking for another entrance, or peeping in windows, they likely would run into more of the beasts and he did not want that at all. They were lucky they came out of the first encounter as well as they did.

"Fine, we approach on the porch, see if we can get a read on what's happening by looking through any windows or cracks there, and proceed with caution." It sounded good, anyway.

"Whatever you say, mister." Ramona didn't really look like she was paying attention. She seemed focused on the house, the weeds, the sounds of the creatures; everything but the area ahead.

Eli and Dakota had to jockey for position to get in front of Ramona and make it to the porch first. She seemed determined to get inside and hopefully rescue her friend, and it was a chore to make sure she didn't herself or anyone else killed from her actions.

As he walked up the few stairs to the porch, Eli noticed the front door seemed to be hanging on by one hinge, leaning askew against the doorframe. He noted it because it would make their entrance a bit easier. Each of his steps made subtle creaking noises that made him cringe a little. The window next to the door was clear, and inside, Eli could see the main room with some junk furniture, and other trash strewn around. In the middle of the room, a large man sat with a gun by his side on the crumpled couch. He looked half asleep, and if Eli was right, he had a number of bandages across his midsection.

Eli turned to Dakota. "One suspect, armed, on a sofa in the center of the room. He definitely came out of the bank. I don't see anyone else around."

"Think he's the last one standing?" Dakota asked.

"Where's Ollie? Do you see him?" Ramona pushed forward to have a look for herself. "He's not there, is he?"

"I'm sure he's alright," Dakota said. "He could be anywhere in this big place."

A sound from inside made the three of them duck away from the window, in time to avoid a man walking by. They initially just saw the man's shadow cast by whatever light was inside, but after he passed, Eli got a look at him, confirming it was another one of the people he saw run out of the bank.

"There's two of them." Dakota nodded. "Now, what happened to the rest?"

That was the question. Where they posted around the house to watch for police? Did they leave as part of the plan, maybe to get other transportation? Eli doubted the last one, as the whole plan seemed off the cuff and off the rails from the moment the bank robbery went wrong.

"Do we go in?" Dakota asked.

Ramona grumbled. "You two think too much." Before they could stop her, the woman bowled in, shoulder first, through the door. The single hinge gave way and the door thudded to the ground.

The door thudded to the ground before Eli knew what was happening. Almost immediately, Dakota pushed forward, past Eli and Ramona, sweeping her shotgun to cover the room. By the time Eli got in, the two subjects within were shouting and moving for cover.

Eli immediately identified the man on the couch as Hank from the mug shots Gino sent. He was in bad shape and moving slowly. The front of the man's shirt was covered in blood from the chest down, but he still grabbed a gun and moved around the couch.

The other man in the room had to have been Stan Dodd. He was a bit more mobile and ducked into a doorway, using the frame for cover.

The room was sparse, with little furniture other than smashed chairs and broken floorboards, so Eli dropped to the ground as Dakota slid behind what was left of a coffee table and chair. Ramona stood straight and let loose with a blast from her shotgun which made even the wounded man move a little quicker.

"Hank Marx? I'm agent Millet with the F.B.I. Drop your weapons and come out with your hands up." Eli noted the brother and sister were missing, as well as the kidnapped boy, Ollie. "Let's not make this worse than it already is." Eli gripped his pistol as he crawled toward Ramona to pull her down out of sight.

Stan responded by firing wildly from his position. Eli saw the man's hand appear with the gun and take three shots without ever looking.

Ramona fired her shotgun again, leaving a series of holes in the wall near where Stan's head would be.

"We just want to know if everyone's alright," Eli said. "Is the boy nearby? Is he injured?"

No one replied this time, with gunfire or otherwise.

Eli crawled to Ramona and grabbed her arm. "Get down here before they clip you."

"Hell with that." Ramona racked the shotgun at the couch and fired, the impact sending filthy fabric and splinters flying.

15

Lana began climbing the rotten stairs quickly, carelessly. She knew the thing had sensed her or smelled her or whatever the grotesque beasts did to scan their surroundings.

"Take my hand," Ollie shouted. He'd made it more than halfway up the tall set of stairs and reached back toward her. Unfortunately, they were too far apart and she couldn't reach him.

A splintered board gave way beneath Lana's feet and her leg went with it. A searing pain went down her calf "Damn it," Lana said. She hung on with her hands, straining to not fall backward down the stairs into the mass of broken junk and whatever else gathered there in the darkness.

"Lana?" Her brother appeared at the top of the stairs. "Are you two okay?" He stepped down gingerly and grabbed Ollie and pulled him up to the top.

Invigorated by the appearance of her sibling, Lana pulled herself back up above the step that gave way. "We're fucking great. Just. Fucking. Great." She glanced down at her leg, covered in blood from what looked to be a nail sticking out of the side of the stairs.

She took a deep breath and reached for the next handhold to get herself out of the basement. A noise behind her made her realize her time was short. She slowly turned her head to look, afraid any sudden change in direction might make another piece of wood come loose.

There, the hulking form she was trying so desperately to escape stood peering up the staircase. She got a better glimpse than before, aided by what light shone down from the light Danny brought. It looked like the smaller ones, only amped up and jacked with muscles. Where the smaller ones had thin wiry arms, this one had virtual tree trunks. Its head, while still covered in wispy hair, looked like a rock, bumpy and rigid.

"The fuck is that? It's even uglier than the rest of them." Danny shone his light at the beast, and red eyes glared back. Many red eyes. As the big creature grabbed onto a hole in the wall to pull himself up, several of the smaller skunk apes howled and hissed as they tried to find a way around it.

Danny drew his gun and shouted, "Get down." to his sister, who barely had time to react before he fired a shot.

"Stop," Lana said. "You're going to hit me." She turned back and couldn't tell if her brother had actually hit the thing or not, but it seemed unfazed, digging for ways to pull itself along the steps.

In the meantime, one of the smaller, lighter skunk apes made it past and crawled along easily, digging its nails into the rotting wood as it went.

Ollie shouted "Look out."

She knew he meant well, but Lana could see the foul thing approaching and could feel its stench enfold her. She carefully turned and kicked at the thing, trying to disrupt its grip. Unfortunately, the thing managed to grab her ankle with one wet hand and pulled her. She instantly felt her already tenuous grip slip from the board ahead.

Danny's hand suddenly was around her wrist and she became the toy in the middle of a tug of war. When one pulled, the other tugged harder.

Meanwhile, the larger creature was making strides and advancing ever closer.

"Danny," Lana said. She wasn't sure what to tell him to do, as they seemed evenly matched and she'd be torn apart if both sides pulled harder. "Shoot it. You're close enough to hit it."

"But…"

"You're right here, you won't hit me."

Lana saw her brother was reluctant to try again.

Behind Danny, Ollie stepped forward and pulled the gun from Danny's waistband. He pushed the man to one side and aimed for a second before shooting the thing square in the face when it looked up. It gurgled once and fell backward, breaking through a particularly rotten area of the stairs and fell out of sight.

Lana felt her brother yank her upward quickly, pulling her so hard she left the steps she was on and nearly ran into Ollie. The three of them didn't linger, finishing their ascent and stepping into the hall above. As they paused there, Ollie held out the gun he'd taken and waited for Danny to take it.

"I occasionally have to take care of predators around our traps. I usually use an old-fashioned six-shooter, but this one is nice too," Ollie said.

"Why are you giving it back?" Lana felt her arms shake a little from all of the climbing and her nerves kicking in.

"If I come walking out with it, your partners will likely shoot me. I'd like to avoid that."

He wasn't wrong, and Lana knew it. It was hard to say what state the others were in back at the main room. Still, if it was her, she might have considered keeping it. It was a bargaining chip at the very least. Maybe he could have shot his way out of the house or something.

Danny took his gun back and nodded at the kid before turning back to the stairs and unleashing the rest of his clip at the huge thing still climbing up. This time, Lana was sure he hit, as the beast flinched with every one of the four shots. But once Danny was done, the creature looked up with angry red eyes propelled itself forward, growling as it climbed without care, feet occasionally falling through broken steps, but grasping a new foothold almost immediately.

"Shit," Lana said. "Let's go." Ahead, she heard more gunshots, maybe shotguns, but she didn't care, she only wanted to get out of the way of what was charging in their direction.

16

There was a sudden commotion from Stan's direction. It sounded more like a stampede than more gunfire. Dakota noticed it, too and turned to Eli. The pair exchanged confused looks before the three missing pieces of the bank robbery puzzle came charging down the hall, making no effort to conceal themselves. Even stranger, they were led by their kidnapping victim, Ollie.

"Freeze," Eli shouted. He rose to one knee and pointed his gun at the doorway. But the trio kept coming, passing where Stan ducked for cover.

"Ollie," Ramona shouted.

The boy looked confused for a moment, but kept running, making a slight course correction to move toward Ramona. "Don't shoot."

Before he could get to her, Hank stood and grabbed him by the arm, stopping his momentum and pointed the gun at him. "Everyone get back or I'll kill him."

The sudden shift in the dynamic of the room through Eli into crisis mode. He needed to disarm the girl and her brother, and deal with the suspects without the kid in the equation. The thing that confused him was the sounds in the hall continued, despite the fact the suspects from the bank job was in the room or nearby. Somehow the rumbling was even louder.

"Drop the gun, Hank. You don't want to make this worse." Dakota had moved to cover the other two who had entered the room while Eli concentrated on rescuing the boy.

"No, I'm not going to jail here. You need to drop your guns before I kill this kid."

Out in the hall, Stan shouted suddenly and came running into the room, gun in hand, but looking behind him.

The sound of the rumbling followed him in the form of a quartet of the skunk apes ambling along with angry purpose. And trailing them, another creature which somewhat resembled them but was markedly different in size and physique. It was much larger and bleeding from some wound lost in the filthy hair covering it.

As Eli took it in, Danny reloaded his gun and started shooting at the things.

Stan turned to fire his gun as well, but was tackled by two of the beasts, who took him to the ground and slashed at him with sinewy arms and mud-caked claws. He fired shots randomly, causing everyone in the room to duck a little out of fear of being hit.

One of the skunk apes barked in pain and fell back away from Stan, a sizable chunk missing from its thigh. It stumbled and fell several feet away. The remaining creature continued to slash at Stan's face until the larger beast caught up and lifted Stan by his leg.

Eli shot at the massive beast, hitting with two shots before the thing roared and slammed Stan against the nearby wall, face-first. The suspect shouted in agony before the beast slammed him against it again, this time, crashing the man through the crumbling plaster and wood and into the next room.

Eli was stunned by the thing's strength, and more so by its ability to shrug off bullets.

"Get that thing away from me," Hank shouted. He turned his gun away from Ollie, and shot at the larger beast.

In a moment of opportunity, Ollie punched Hank in the side, causing more blood to ooze from the bandages. As the big man screamed in pain, Ollie ran and moved toward Ramona as quickly as he could.

In the midst of the chaos, Dakota fired her shotgun, knocking Hank to the ground, shouting in agony. Seconds after he hit the floor, the big hairy beast was on him, pounding the man with both fists, swinging its limbs down on him in unison, resulting in a bloody crackling sound that ended Hank's screams with a wet gurgle which stretched into a hiss of expelled air.

"Over by the back wall," Lana shouted. "Ollie and I fell through that hole to the basement. Maybe we can get it to fall in the hole, too. The whole area is pretty fucked. At least it'll get it away from us."

Eli noted the hole when they came in, but quickly forgot it as soon as everything went to hell. It certainly hadn't entered his mind it might be the key to saving his life at some point later in the day.

He tried to focus on the monstrosity in front of him, but Eli's gaze kept drifting to the hallway where new skunk apes trickled in every minute. The air smelled like the stinging scent of smoke from the gunfire, and the room was alive with the shouts and whoops of the strange creatures. As he neared the gaping hole in the floor, he stopped to let off three more rounds into the thing, only to be frustrated at the lack of reaction from it.

Behind the beast, he could see the others struggling with the rest of the skunk apes. Ramona seemed fine as she bashed one of the things in the skull with the butt of her shotgun, blood splattering across the floor as she did. He was momentarily shocked when he saw Ollie with a gun, likely Stan or Hank's. But as the situation had devolved as it had, it was everyone from themselves.

"Eli, watch out," Dakota shouted. In his amazement at the situation and his constant reassessment of what the hell was going on, Eli failed to focus on the big creature right in front of him. Out of nowhere, the creature's thick right arm slammed into Eli, knocking him to the ground. His skull throbbed immediately, blurring his vision. He pushed himself up onto his elbows, trying to get himself back on his feet, but the strength had drained out of his body, making every action agony. As the beast approached, Eli realized he had not escaped from it. If he ran, it would be either right at the monster, or right along the dangerous rim of the raggedy hole in the floor. With each step the thing took, Eli could hear the floor creak and feel it give in just a bit more under the massive thing's weight.

17

It seemed the waves of disgusting skunk apes would never stop. Each time Lana shoved one away or killed it, another two would take her place. She'd run out of ammunition quickly and resorted to broken table legs and fists to keep herself alive. She'd taken a nasty swipe across her shoulder and a bite on the leg, but she wouldn't let herself stop, not while her brother was still struggling to live as well.

Danny shoved off one of the things and ran to her. "You still okay?" He was also bloody and torn.

"Not really. You?"

"Nope."

"Uncle Hank is gone. Has to be, the way those things got him," Lana said. It was a fact that came out, not an emotional declaration or tearful remembrance. She didn't know if it was the insane situation, or her growing resentment of Hank's influence over her life, but she didn't feel anything for the man. She was just reporting the news to her brother.

"Yeah." A skunk ape leapt at him and he stabbed it with a pointed spindle from the staircase, driving it into the things' neck as both fell to the floor in a flurry of punching, biting and stabbing.

Quickly turning, Lana kicked the creature, connecting hard with its midsection, giving Danny a chance to stab it once more, this time in the throat, causing a sudden eruption of blood from the wound.

"Fuck," Danny said, shoving the beast off of him and wiping blood from his face.

Around them, the chaos still ensued, though it momentarily avoided them. Nearby, the largest of the beasts closed on one of the agents. The man looked on the verge of passing out, struggling to avoid the advancing monster. It was hard to tell if he knew how close he was to the massive hole she and Ollie had fallen through in the floor.

At the other end of the room, the front door lay in splinters on the ground. The doorway was unobstructed and none of the agents were close enough to it to block them. There had to be at least one boat out there that worked. If she and her brother could make it outside, they'd be home free. If they didn't go now, they'd be the only ones left from the bank robbery, and they'd be the ones to take all the blame for it. They'd take the heat for the killings, the robbery, the kidnapping.

"Let's get out of here," she said. Her brother looked around the room and then at her. She couldn't quite read the look on his face, other than overwhelming exhaustion. "What?"

Over near the hallway, Ramona bashed a skunk ape in the head with the butt of her shotgun as she let out an exclamation into the air as wild as anything the beasts had let loose with.

"Maybe we need to stay and help?" Danny got himself to his feet.

"We'll be arrested."

"Jesus, everything that happened today, and you're thinking we're running away? Where are we going to go? I'm too exhausted to run."

"We're going to jail. We'll take the blame for all of it." Lana said. "That's some insane jail time. If we get hit with those murders, we're never leaving prison. It would be stupid *not* to try to run now."

Her brother shook his head. "These people could die because of us, too. I can't have that on me." Without another word to her, he charged at the huge creature near the agent and slammed squarely into its back. The beast easily maintained its balance, though it was distracted enough to swing it's long arms like a helicopter, huge swatting limbs outstretched, glancing off the top of Danny's head and knocking him sideways.

She watched him fall, thinking for a millionth time that day that he was an idiot. The thing seemed bulletproof; how would his charge do anything to it?

"*No!*" Watching her brother drop sent a jolt down her spine. She ran at it too, but instead of trying to tackle it at the waist, she aimed for the legs, hoping to buckle its knees as she charged.

As she approached it, the floor let out a loud crackle of protest and something below her snapped and crumbled. She felt more of the floor give way.

"Shit, get away from the hole. It's all going to go." Her momentum got her close to the beast, but she didn't run into it as she'd planned. Instead, she reached out for her brother. "Come on, Danny."

Stubbornly, her brother shrugged her off and stepped back toward the huge skunk ape.

His run was halted as the old woman shot at the floor around the monster's feet. "If this thing laughs off bullets to the chest, what makes you think you can punch it and hurt it?" She racked her shotgun again and fired another volley, shredding the wood.

18

Eli saw what the woman was doing and decided to help by shooting at the beast's face, hoping to get it to back up and further onto the weak area.

After two shots that landed somewhere near the creature's eyes, Eli's gun ran dry. His slide locked forward, indicating he was out. He'd used his extra clips already and had no more ammunition stashed to fall back on. The creature stumbled, as Eli had hoped, and an additional shot from Ramona brought about the last straw. The huge skunk ape stepped backward, stimulated by the sensation on its feet, as the floor finally gave up and snapped, dropped the floor out of place quickly.

The skunk ape swung its long arms for balance, trying to save itself, but couldn't and dropped almost in slow motion into the widening crevice.

A second later the beast shrieked as it landed in the basement with a crash.

Eli crawled to the edge, side-by-side with Lana, and looked down into the hole, careful of their footing, mindful of each creak of the floorboards below. The beast had fallen into a room filled with metal and trash, likely thrown there from the heyday of the mansion. Eli pulled his flashlight and shined it down. The beam reflected off of glass and other junk around the beast's broken body. Based on the fight with the thing, he guessed it would have survived the fall, but its body was riddled with shards of metal sticking through it, protruding from the neck and chest.

The handful of skunk apes left in the room slowed their frenzy of attacks after the giant fell through the floor. They waved their arms, and whooped in unison while slowly backing away toward the hall and off into the darkness there.

It was just as well. Eli was out of ammunition, and it looked like Dakota switched to using her shotgun as a club. Ramona and Ollie were punching and swinging anything they could find at the creatures. The two suspects, the brother and sister, didn't seem to have weapons either. All in all, Eli was thrilled to see the things go.

"Let's go," Ramona grumbled. "I'm not up for chasing those things around this house playing god damn hide and seek."

As Eli tried to reply, he was interrupted by a low rumble outside. It was barely audible enough to register with him, like a bug zipping past his ear.

"The hell is that?"

Dakota said, "I heard it, too. More of these things?"

"Can't be. God, it's not possible, is it?"

Ramona shuffled for the door. "Ridiculous. That's a helicopter, probably three, actually. You need to listen to the thud of the rotors." She grabbed Ollie and yanked him along with her.

19

The rumble outside got louder as Eli followed Ramona out. He'd picked up a stubby leg of the couch and made his way to the space where the front door once hung on its frame. The instant he did so, the area lit up as though it was the middle of the day. Eli raised his hand to shield his eyes. But even then, he could tell the lights came from the sky in front of him and to his left, from spotlights mounted on helicopters. He couldn't tell if there were two or three of them, but they managed to illuminate all of the little island in front of him.

It took a second for him to realize Dakota was standing beside him, holding her shotgun like a club. "Cavalry?" She asked.

"I think that would imply they were here just in time to save us, not to clean up the mess we left."

The lights swept away, scanning other parts of the island as Ramona pushed past Eli and Dakota, nearly dragging Ollie behind her.

"Whoa, Ramona, wait. We don't know if there might be a few of these things still creeping around," Eli said. "At least let us go with you." He hurried to keep up, but failed, too exhausted to match the energy of the older woman.

"Bah." The woman waved him off.

At the edge of the trees, near Ramona's beloved boat, the *Marsh Mellow*. One of the helicopters made a small circle before landing partially in the water. a trio of men in tactical gear leapt out of the one side of the copter, splashing mud and swamp water as they landed. They quickly charged into the weeds; assault weapons ready.

On the other side, three people in dark blue suits stepped out onto the sandy shore and glanced around before walking toward Ramona and Ollie. Two women and one decidedly tall man. Eli increased his strides so he could get around the woman and her charge, to intercept what he assumed were

Federal agents here to help them out. Despite Eli's outstretched hand, one of the women stepped around him and hugged Ramona with a sudden grin on her face.

"Thanks for the call, Ramona," the agent said. "Shit got real in a hurry here, didn't it?"

The older woman shrugged. "Nothing like the old days, that's for sure." Ramona pointed to Eli and said, "This one's with the Bureau." She pointed to the woman and said, "This is agent Dearborn. Now we all know each other. She tossed her shotgun into the back of her small boat and folded her arms impatiently. "Whenever you people are done dicking around, I need a ride home. The skunk apes destroyed my dinghy and the fucking crooks fucked up my fishing boat."

Agent Dearborn agreed. "Absolutely. I'll get Mike or Terry to get you back to your palace."

"I don't understand, what do you mean, the old days?" Dakota asked. "You've done this before?"

"Does this look like my first rodeo?" Ramona leaned against the vehicle and smiled. "I've been around."

"Ramona was one of our best agents. Only just retired a few years ago."

"She was an F-B-I agent?" The thought gave Eli a slight pain in his temple. The loudmouth swamp lady likely held a higher position in the bureau than he did?

"Oh, no. We're not with the F-B-I. They didn't want to shoulder the weight of an agency like ours. No, we're part of the Department of Agriculture."

"The Department of Agriculture? You chase little monsters around the swamp for the Department of Agriculture?" The pain in his temple throbbed a little more.

A group of airboats approached and beached themselves nearby, more men in tactical gear disembarked and started around the island.

"We chase all kinds of things around all sorts of places, Agent Millet." Dearborn said. "We get a nice budget under APHIS and no one asks too many questions."

Millet wiped the sweat from his brow and smiled. He knew APHIS was Agriculture's Animal and Plant Health Inspection Service, and the sheer balls it took for the government to hide an agency that hunted monsters under the guise of animal inspection made him laugh out loud. Behind him, he heard Dakota snort as she got the joke as well.

Eli held his hands up in surrender to the absurdity of the whole conversation. "Great. You get a gold star for the day. Since we also lost our ride, we'll need help getting our prisoners back to dry land and warm jail cells."

"I can't even imagine the paperwork this is going to take," Dakota said. She looked around at the agents who'd appeared from the helicopters and boats, in hip waders and blue windbreakers that covered the scene like ants. "These are all your people, aren't they?"

Dearborn nodded.

"So, no other agency is here? How are we going to explain this? Nobody in my precinct believes in bigfoot or skunk apes or little green men, so how do we write this in a report?"

Eli laughed again. He was exhausted, achy and wanted nothing more than to go home. Unfortunately, Dakota was right, they had debriefs, reports and some intense scrutiny ahead of them. They had to talk about their pursuit of the bank robbers, the shootout in front of the bank, Ollie's kidnapping, their involvement of a civilian as far as Ramona was concerned, the story she's not a civilian, but instead a former government agent, and then there's the matter of their contact with a horde of unknown creatures, and the subsequent battle with them that led to the murder and mauling of two of the robbery suspects, and the capture of two other suspects. And the rescue of the kidnap victim. And the backup from an obscure department of the federal government. Did that cover it? Eli was sure there were more points to the past twenty-four hours, but he was too tired to nitpick.

"Someone grabbed the money, right?" Dakota asked. "I mean, just checking. I'd be happy to hold on to it, if it's just going to rot in the swamp."

Agent Dearborn gave a small smile. "We remembered to pick that up."

"Just asking. I have loans and a mortgage."

Eli watched as a half a dozen officers carried the body of the largest skunk ape past him on the way to the nearby helicopter.

"You guys took out the king or some shit," agent Dearborn said. "Thing's bigger than any I've ever seen, that's for sure. You're lucky to be alive."

"Pssst," Ramona blew a raspberry from the nearby boat and waved the agent off. "Luck. You know me better than that. Skill. It was all skill. I would have been done sooner if it wasn't for these meddling kids."

Eli exchanged a confused look with Dakota. "Does she think we're the kids?" Eli smiled, knowing he was on the young side of his forties, and there was no way he was asking Dakota her age but he figured she'd barely cleared her twenties. As he stood aching and bleeding from the events of the past twenty-four hours, he surely didn't feel like a kid. Not one bit.

"What's going to happen to the kid and her brother?" Dakota asked.

"Well, they robbed a bank and their gang shot and killed two people today. I'd say they're going to jail for a few days, after a stint in the hospital," Erickson said.

"They also saw some serious shit today. Fucking skunk ape riot, their uncle met an untimely and ugly demise," Eli tried to muster up every ounce of sympathy for them he could. It sounded like they'd been sucked into the criminal life by someone they trusted at one time. Still, he couldn't help but think about today's crimes, and the other bank robberies in other states the crew had committed.

As the huge ape king was loaded on the helicopter and the door slid shut, Danny said "We're not riding with that thing, are we?"

"It's dead." Eli used the best authoritative voice he could muster.

"Is it?" Lana asked

"Yes."

"Do you want to ride with it?" Lana asked.

Eli turned to keep the wash from the helicopter from blowing in his face. "Hell no. I'd rather walk."

Eli and Dakota walked with Lana and Danny to a waiting airboat nearby and helped them aboard. The four of them sat on the long bench-like seats, but none of them turned their backs on the house. While Eli watched, he noticed a small fire erupt, visible from one of the busted downstairs windows. Quickly, the flames became visible through another window and seemed to grow higher.

"Uh, Erickson? Dearborn? There's a…"

"You didn't think we were going to just pack everything up and go home to study it, did you?" Erickson looked grim in the faint work lights of the other agents.

Dearborn agreed, "Shit, you're trained law enforcement officers and you were lucky to get out alive. Imagine if some dumbass tourist boat got too close to this little kingdom of skunk apes. It'd be tragic."

"So, what does this agency do then? I assumed you were out to study this weird shit," Eli asked.

"Well. We do study these phenomena, but only inasmuch as how they impact the average citizen and the security of the United States," Dearborn said. "But…"

As the agent continued, her voice was completely obscured by the roar and growl of the huge fans at the back of the swamp boat. And though the agent continued her explanation, Eli was sure she knew whatever classified details she was conveying were lost to the racket.

The lack of explanation was okay with Eli, at least for the moment. His head ached from the events of the day. Whatever help these agents from the Biological Incongruities Office could offer seemed like a long way away from explaining how two wanted fugitives were killed and nearly devoured by creatures from the swamp. He was having a tough time piecing it all together himself.

As their boat slowly pulled away from the mucky island, Ramona and Ollie waved at them with an odd enthusiasm. Eli waved back, but with less excitement. Not far behind the odd pair, the old house had already begun to surrender to the flames. The upper floors were burning, flames emerged from the basement. But as dead as the old thing was, Eli was still sure more of the strange beasts would come flooding out at any moment to attack and devour the agents that dotted the shore.

He relaxed a little as they picked up speed, but couldn't quite bring himself to look away from the flames, vigilant for whatever might emerge.

Agent Eli Millett and Trooper Dakota Irwin will return in the next *Cryptid Pursuit* adventure:

Mothman Autopsy

More books by author Matt Betts

White Anvil: Sasquatch Onslaught

Fleeing an approaching blizzard, a military train carrying prisoners and a handful of citizens derails in the mountains. The survivors fight to stay alive and regroup as the terrible storm buries them in snow. Only then do they discover the train also carried another cargo—two cars loaded with biological experiments—genetically-altered sasquatches conditioned to annihilate anything they find.

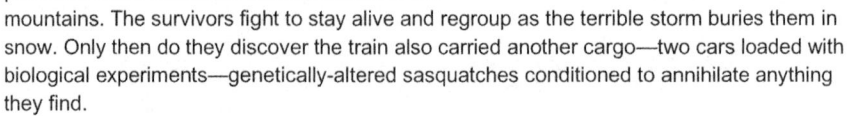

Can the few remaining soldiers team with a pair of sisters and a police constable to fight the relentless beasts, icy temperatures, and escaped prisoners long enough for help to arrive?

"Cryptid lovers rejoice, for you have found the author who will lead you to an action-packed adventure that you will ignore family to read." — Jonathan Lazar, Author of Zachariah Lars and the High Elf Mystery

"For those of us who grew up on Saturday morning creature features and painstakingly tuned-in to horror hosts using our dented and bent rabbit-ear antennas, Matt Betts delivers all the goods and more. WHITE ANVIL is packed with the excitement and atmosphere, but it also has what so many stories lack: Believable characters behaving rationally as they do their best to survive in the face of unexpected terror. — Dan Stout author of Titanshade

ASIN : B07ZS89P51   **Publisher : Severed Press**

Indelible Ink

It's What's Inside That Counts

Something lurks inside Deena Riordan. She never once questioned her life in the criminal underworld as the star of Mr. Marsh's illegal empire and his youngest assassin. Her ruthless demeanor and dark magical powers have kept her at the top of the heap for years. But one day she pushes the sorcery too far and something snaps. Only then does Deena realize she's always been a puppet of that dark power with no true will of her own.

Now, in order to get out of the crime business for good, she needs to save her sister from Marsh's angry clutches. It won't be easy. She'll have to make her way through friends turned foes, dodge determined federal agents, and stay out of a particularly stubborn fellow hitman's sights. Worst of all, Deena will have to wrestle with the darkness inside to keep it from swallowing her up again.

ASIN : B00VEFD5YS   **Publisher : Dog Star Books**

MORE MATT

Website
mattbetts.com

Amazon.com Page
https://amzn.to/3m6l8rW

- find more books by Matt
- *leave a review*
- ask a question

Printed in Great Britain
by Amazon